WESTWARD
TO LAUGHTER

Colin MacInnes

WESTWARD TO LAUGHTER

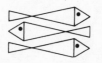

Farrar, Straus & Giroux
New York

For
Francis Wyndham

Contents

The Harbour

I T W A S just past my sixteenth birthday that I first learned about the world; and this from my uncle Zachary, molasses chandler in the port of Mortar which, to we lads in Ayrshire then, seemed like some Babylon or Rome. To him I had come on foot in desperate condition from the Clearances, bearing oatmeal on my back, and with only to recommend me to him my honest youth, my faith in the predestined doctrine (for my dominie had early rescued me from the Popish errors of my poor slaughtered Father), and the hope he would acknowledge all the fondness and respect towards her Lowland brother that my dear lost Mother had enjoined upon me as she lay split-hearted in the exile of the glens.

'Aye, aye, aye,' said uncle Zachary, observing me pin-eyed on my distressed arrival. 'Aye, aye – but it all comes of her going to a Highlander, as I warned.'

I bowed my head: seeking to show my good uncle Zachary with humble patience, yet with simple pride, that though I admitted all the wasted errors of the defeated Celts, yet it was by my Mother's own choice of lover that I had been made myself in part one.

'Aye, aye', he continued. 'But your dominie, at least, told you the good word?'

'Indeed, uncle,' I replied. 'For the Word had spread north into our quarter of the Highlands; and besides, no Papist there was scholar enough to teach us bairns.'

'Aye,' he said. 'Tell me your Catechism, boy.' I did so without fault. 'Your multiplication tables up to 20 times 20,' and this also I performed by perfect rote.

'Aye,' he said, 'Alexander *Nairn*' (spitting out my father's name), and I saw no more of him till kirk on Sunday.

Now that I am older, being past eighteen and a man, I know well how foolishly, and in what ill light, a young lad may present himself to those of riper years. This indeed, as I lie waiting my End here in the furthest Tropicks, is the chief sorrowful reflection that consumes my remaining days. For had I, as a lad in Mortar, possessed the maturity to persuade my uncle Zachary that I was ill equipped for the voyage that he offered me, and which I embarked upon with such eager ignorance, I might happily have remained in Ayrshire there honestly to live out my days in modest regularity. But such, two years past, was my impetuous ardour, and my fatal desire to please, that my doom was sealed the very day I embarked from Mortar for the West Indies.

The trade in molasses, which was the chief staple of my Uncle's commerce, depended upon his correspondence with merchants across the border in the ports of Liverpool and Bristol; and it may well be my Uncle's close association with the trade in slaves and sugar that had encouraged him in his support of the Union and in his hatred of the rebellions against the Hanoverians in which my poor Father lost his life. Yet I would not then believe that any brother to my dear Mother could be actuated only by the thought of gain. For it is certain also that in all his enterprises my uncle Zachary was equally impelled by the desire to nourish Presbyterian culture in the Lowlands, and to bring civilisation to the barbarous islands of the West Indies.

After some months learning the simpler basics of his commerce by day, and studying texts and mathematicks with the Minister by candlelight, my Uncle called me to his countinghouse at dawn one morning, and told me to look out at a barque lying hanging by the quay. 'Yon's your hame, lad,' he said, pointing to the vessel, 'and yon, I might say, is the academy that will instruct ye in the right ways of commerce and the world. Step abroad now, Alexander, and enquire for the Master, Mr Peters, who's expectin' ye. And may the Lord bless and prosper ye, as much for his ane guid sake as for your puir daft mither's.' Then, masking his emotions, he embraced me, and gave me, as parting gifts, a book of Precepts by John Calvin writ in Latin, a half flask of malt whisky wrapped round by brass, and in a leather purse with thongs, my Mother's part of their joint inheritance which, I found with rapture when I opened it, amounted to no less than four whole guineas.

On reaching the quay, I asked to be conveyed to Captain Peters, and was ushered up on board by an honest seaman who took me to the door of a small cabin on the poop. On this I knocked more than once until a voice, in the first English speech I had yet heard in my young lifetime, called out to me in a muffled way, 'Fuck off!'

It must not be thought that Scots lads, though certainly chaster in their tongues than those of England, are of such innocence as not to know the rougher words that men use among men. But even so, I was surprised, as I stood there rocking gently with my small possessions in the mist, that such a greeting should be uttered, even to a raw lad like myself, by one in such authority as Mr Peters. But always, in my boyhood, my Mother had enjoined upon me that courtesy and patience which, fortified by prayer, can steadfastly withstand rough buffets; and I therefore knocked upon the door once more and said, 'Captain Peters, sir, 'tis I.'

There was a crash within like the burn tumbling down the boulders, and the door wrenched open to disclose a figure whom I took to be my new Master. He peered at me through eyes blinking with, no doubt, the toil on his night watches, and perceiving my whisky bottle, he seized and drained it in a gulp. Then grabbing me by the shoulder he pulled me inside his den, whose condition surprised me greatly as I had always supposed ships' cabins to be light and aery; whereas this one was dark and foul. First lighting a lamp with wandering fingers, the Captain subsided on his tousled bunk, while I stood in calm respect, awaiting his commands. For a while he gazed at me in silence, blinking, then said, 'Fucking arse-holes.'

'Sir,' I replied, 'I bid you a hearty good morning.'

'Would you believe it,' said the Captain.

'Sir,' I continued, 'I am instructed by my uncle Zachary to present myself to you for such employment on your vessel as you will deem fitting for my full instruction in the art of commercial navigation.'

'Woad!' the Master yelled.

There appeared now a Figure such as I had never beheld before, though dimly heard of, namely a Negro of alarming aspect. This Creature was some seven feet in his height, and broad in all proportions; with a countenance so distorted and villainous as to confirm by his very person the dread curse that was laid upon the loins of Ham. He stood there half bent (since the cabin was no taller than I was), with his huge arms all dangling horribly, and his fingers clutching at the air; and on his face, in the dim lustre, a diabolical expression in which malice and mockery were equally imprinted.

'Wheel him away, Woad,' said the Captain.

'Aye, aye, skip,' Woad replied.

Then grasping me, to my indignation, as if I were some sack or bundle, this Monster propelled me stumbling along the deck towards a noisome shaft in the rear portion of the ship. Down this I tumbled, where I found myself to be in a narrow box, or hold, in which by the scent and snores it was apparent that others invisible were slumbering.

'Welcome aboard, boy,' said this Woad.

'"Boy"!' I cried. 'To whom do you thus address yourself, blackguard?'

Woad let out a horrid laugh that reverberated round the foetid box. 'He, he, he,' he cried, 'you beat my time.'

He vanished, then came bearing a beaker of some dark fluid and what, in the dim light, I took to be a brick. 'Eat, drink and be merry, boy,' said Woad, seating himself at the bench and gazing at me.

But I was too out of countenance to do so, and was hotly shamed that a tear started in my eye, which fortunately for my honour the savage did not observe.

'Now lissen, boy,' said Woad. 'Firs question: you play whopee?'

'Do I play what?'

'Is like a game: with card an' ting.'

'God forbid,' I cried, 'that I should have commerce with the Devil's Picture Book.'

'Hé, well, you not need no money, will you, till we reach the Wes' Indies, see, so you make me a loan, now, for the viage.'

13

Before I could reply, his long arm had shot out and grasped the purse that held my inheritance close to my bosom, and his hand fast disappeared in the recesses of his tattered garments. 'Jus' like a loan, see,' he said smiling, 'an' maybe I cut you in the profit, boy, cos this Woad here, he's a winner.'

It was by now sadly apparent to me that since Captain Peters had placed me in the clutches of this Animal, it behoved me to act prudently until such time as I could escape from the horrid situation: a plan for performing which was already maturing in my mind. I made therefore no complaint about the money, feeling sure that, in due time, the Captain would restore it to me, and punish the Hottentot for his presumption; and I meanwhile decided that a superior intelligence would enable me to elicit from this simple Brobdignagian the information that would aid me in my intent.

'So you are Mr Woad,' I said to him.

'"Mister"? Oh, tank you, boy. But "Woad" will do, you know: jus' Woad.'

'And so, Woad, you are an African?'

'Hé, hé, hé! Me? No, man. That was my ancestors. Me, boy, I from the sweet island of St Laughter.'

I was unacquainted with that saint, and told him so.

'Well no,' he said, 'is perhaps not a real saint name, proper like, but is a name we give it to the island, cos it so joyful an' melodious, you see.'

'So you were born there?'

'Yes, man, there in St Laughter: though who my daddy is, I could never tell you.'

'But then, Mr Woad . . .'

'Hé now – don't you mamagai me with all that "Mister". Why I mus' tell you twice?'

'Yes, well then, Woad – why are you not a slave?'

Woad let out a bellow so loud that there were lamentations from the sleeping sailors. 'Hé, hé!' he cried. 'I not disappoint you, boy! I *is* a slave.'

'Then why are you on this ship? Where are your shackles?'

'Shackle! So you want me in chains, boy? But tell me, now: how I goin' to climb that riggin' with me sparklin' chains on, do you say? How I goin' to navigate or anyting?'

'But you might escape!'

'Escape? Where to, now? To sweet Scotland here? You see me walkin' up the levee, in you little harbour, saying, "Here I is, people – Woad – please bid me welcome"?'

'No.'

'Well – no, like you say. Where I escape to, tell me? Back to Africa? I never seen it, even.'

'Mr Peters' ship does not sail there?'

'No, man. Wes' Indies to Bristol carrying sugar, Bristol to Indies carrying slaves.'

'From Africa.'

'Ah – you got it now. They sail them up north to Bristol then we sail them out westwards to St Laughter.'

I reflected. 'But then, Woad,' I asked, 'what do *you* do in all this?'

'Me? Well, I like the ole family retainer. I welcome they Africans on board, and see them safe across the broad Atlantic to their destiny.'

'And then they become like you?'

'Eggsackly: you clever, boy, I see!'

He waited, so I continued: 'And are there many on the ship, Woad, like yourself?'

'No, man – I unique. The rest here is all Bukra men,

civilise like yourself. Is only me the ignorant savage here to help you take they Africans to a happier land . . . you know? Like when you want to catch wild goat, you put a tame goat in a pen, so the wild ones they come quieter.'

The uncouth utterances of this simple fellow, tainted with ignorance and prejudice though they were, had on me in the weak moment of an unripe age, a saddening effect; and it needed all the faith with which I had been fortified by my dear Mother, my sagacious dominie, and by the true light that shines upon the Elect from the divine lamp of Predestination, to strengthen me against the Devil's voice which, in the shape of the demon Woad, was whispering insidiously into my young ear. Let it not, even in fell confusion or in direst tribulation, ever be for a second doubted! Man is born good, or born to evil – there is no other. If good, through the Fall of our First Ancestors, he is beset by sin; yet, by Heaven's will, may yet find the path to glory eternal that is promised him. But if born doomed to Evil, there is no hope – no, none! And what greater evil can there be than slavery? To be a creature so far banished from the Light as to be but a creature: a frame with outer lineaments of humanity, however repulsive; yet within, such a Zero as to be the Hall the Evil One will instantly inhabit; and whence he will speak to the Elect with a thousand treacherous tongues!

Such a one, so cursed, I knew, was Woad. But in my horror at his presence and his message, there arose another thought which came to me in that instant from my Father. Child of the Triple Tyrant though he was, I could not believe his violent life was never touched by grace! And had he not said to me, as he lay dying for his sad and hopeless cause, that he fought so that slavery should not come into the High-

lands? And come there soon afterwards it had! For hundreds
of the clansmen, taken prisoner by the English, had been
spared from slaughter for the slave ships. Could these slaves,
my father's blood, be demons too? Heaven forbid! And I consoled myself in this perplexity by remembering that the Highlanders, though carried off in chains, remained, unlike the
Tempter sitting near to me, as white as I.

'Hé, hé,' said Woad. 'Me tink you's ponderin' very deeply.'

I arose. 'May I go up on deck,' I said, 'and learn my way
about this vessel?'

Woad looked at me aslant. 'Now I wonder, boy,' he said,
'if you was tinkin' of doin' anyting so peculiar as to try an' hop
off onto the shore again.' He paused, and my head hung a
little. 'Cos if you was,' he continued, 'I'd have to inform you
that unless you can walk upon the waves, like miracle, you
not be able.'

With a cry, I sprung up the ladder: and saw on the deck, to
my dismay, that Mortar was a mile off, and the hills now
visible beyond. I leapt to the balustrade and jumped: forgetting,
in my frenzied lust to leave this Hell Ship, that I had never
learned to swim.

The Caves

OF MY salvage by a boat hook, the fifty lashes from the Quartermaster, and all my vomiting to Liverpool, I shall say nothing: except that I left Scotland a boy, and reached England something of a man. I soon learned not to speak to Captain Peters, for the first and only time I did so, he slashed me with a spike, needing six yarn stitches. The crew rarely spoke to me, unless to curse; and indeed, what with my sickness and my ignorance, I was nothing but a hindrance to them. Some of them, in the hold, made Attempts upon me which I would not have conceived possible in other than Beasts; but my vomit defended my honour, if not my muscles. Woad ignored me, except to ask, when he lost my four guineas in a rowdy game, if I had not more hidden on my person. As for his fellow seamen, although they addressed him with contumely, they kept a certain distance from him, it appeared.

I was not allowed ashore at Liverpool, where my chief duty in the port was to hoist aboard the seamen lurching back from their debauches. But when we entered the river Avon, nearing Bristol, the Captain sent for me and said, 'You got any brains?'

'Yes, Mr Peters,' I replied.

'Very well, then. I am going to offer you a choice, like – see?'

'Yes, sir?'

'Shaddup. Choice one. Your uncle in Mortar has paid me a

single fare to carry you to the West Indies. What you do there, or do not do, is no business of mine or his. Get me?'

'No, sir.'

'Shaddup, I said. So choice one is, I keep my bargain, carry you there and disembark you – right?'

'What other choice, Captain Peters?'

'Belt up. Choice two, I economise on your passage money by signing you as slop boy on any ship sailing East I can persuade to take you so I do not have to feed you, and you can not get back to Mortar to tell your uncle that I robbed him. What do you say?'

'But Captain Peters, sir, I . . .'

'Fuck me, Charlie! Choice one, or choice two? Answer!'

'I shall stay on the ship, Captain.'

'Oh – will you! Well, there are certain conditions about *that*, and you better hear them. What?'

'Nothing, Captain.'

'Shaddup, then. If you come with me, forget about the passage money – you got to *work*.'

'Yes, sir.'

'Work – not puke. Work. Now here in Bristol, we take niggers on. That needs a rather special kind of seamanship. Well go on – speak up!'

'Yes, sir?'

'"Yes sir"! Are you a sweet tender-hearted boy, are you?'

'Sir, I would beg you . . .'

'Bollocks. Call Woad.'

'Call Woad, sir?'

'Fuck me! Call him!'

When Woad entered the cabin, the Captain handed me a thong. 'Slash him,' he said.

'Slash who, sir?'

'Oh my Gawd! Slash him!' He seized the thong from me and lashed Woad's face twelve times. 'Now you,' he said, handing me the leather.

'No, sir.'

'No? All right. The East Indies for you, not the West. Fuck off.'

'But Captain . . .'

The Captain beat at me and I ran out. Woad, wiping blood out of his eyes, said, 'So you coward, baby?'

'And *you* say . . .'

'Yes – coward. You not hit because you love me? Because you think is bad? No, boy. You not hit because you frighten of what you believe. But you should be brave in what you believe. An' you not hit because you still frighten of *me*.'

'No!'

'Oh, yes. Alone you are, and you dam right to be. Well, let me tell you something. Watch out. Make yourself wicked. Toughen up. Because believe me, out there you *will* be alone some day.'

By this time I had reached my decision. I would not stay on this cursed vessel; nor would I sail perforce to the East Indies; nor dared I return yet to Mortar, since my uncle had betrayed me so. I would make my way off the ship, which in a river must be easier than at sea, and I would try to find in Bristol, or in London if I could reach it, some decent Presbyterian family that might give me honest employment worthy of my modest merits.

Thus, as night fell upon the sluggish stream, I lowered my person down a line and dropped into the shallows underneath the bowsprit. Neck-deep, I laboured to the soupy bank, and clambered up the rocky crag beyond. From the eminence above, I had a prospect of the slaver riding inward with a lazy tide, and set beyond the stream, the fairest sight on earth I had yet encountered. This, spread out in glory, was the port of Bristol: and to me, who had seen yet only Mortar, it seemed a pure grandiloquence: with noble terraces hanging to the skies, and all the pomp of a pink and pearly Metropolis. How glorious was Man, my young heart told me, to have made such a Beauty out of Earth!

In such a generous place, I felt, there would be, even for such a microbe as I was, some fitting posture; and hastening downwards from the crags where I was standing, I sought a road to carry me into the town. When after some half hour of eager travelling, I heard a turmoil horrible to mortal ears: a huge wail and groan of agony.

Hastening fearfully, I beheld the Caves: huge Openings in the red cliffs, lashed across with chains and barricades. At these clutched a hundred fingers, and pressed up at them I saw masks torn in pain and desperation. The yells from within were indescribable: brute cries not human, but appalling. And even from this distance there proceeded, from out of these foul recesses, a stench most loathsome of blood, rotted flesh, foul vomits, heaped ordures. These, I perceived, must be the slaves: and from them I fled with loathing and revulsion.

Calmed somewhat by the pleasurable outskirts of the city, I decided on the harbour as the best place for any reconnaissance; for tho' I knew little of the world, and naught of England, that little I had learned was of the sea; and among the seamen, I could hope, might be encountered some kindly fellow – perhaps even another Scot – who could best advise me in my timid assault upon the town.

Fortune so turned my steps that outside an inn, frequented by mariners and such landsmen as must meet with them – and by some female harpies, too, whose extravagant aspect and demeanour much disturbed me – I saw an old sailor from our ship, called Varco, who was a Cornishman. Among the crew, he was the only sailor who, in my desolate discontent, had spoken to me with some gentility; having, no doubt, that patience with the young which an older man without ambition sometimes confers on youthful inexperience. I hailed this honest salt, and he welcomed me and offered me a glass of ale.

'You did well, lad,' he said, 'to make off as you did. For I have little doubt that Captain Peters's intent was to indent you by chicane on some rotted vessel chartered to the Orient. Moreover, on our own ship, had you stayed with us, you would not have been at all content.'

I asked him why this might be, and the old sailor, pulling on his cob reflectively (and spitting thoughtful dollops on the cobbles), thus enlightened me:

'You see, lad, I have for many years been engaged with Slavers: on the Atlantic run, such as we now intend, and also, in my younger days, along the coasts of Africa. The commerce is an honest one and, with a worthy Captain, the crews benefit by bonuses from the Planters. Nor is it difficult, so far as cargo handling is concerned; for as you can imagine, lad, 'tis easier far to put a man on board, in shackles with the lash, than is the labour of loading sacks of grains or minerals. As for the sea passage itself, except for the stench, and the nuisance of toppling into the sea the corpses that occur, there is little to it: the wails, save for sea sickness, soon diminish, and violence need not be feared when chains and whips are handy.'

'But is there not,' I asked, 'some peril when the slaves are first put aboard the ship? For surely, brutes though they are, they do not embark easily upon their travels.'

'That is scarcely an affair,' the mariner replied. 'For at the harbours of the Coast, where the slaves are sold to us, they have first been taken, and then tamed, by European factors, who purchase them from Africans that raid into the inland tribes, and trade the black bodies captured for grog and muskets which the factors offer them.'

'But have these Africans,' I asked, 'no scruple to consign their fellows to the factors?'

The old sailor smiled. 'I recall,' he answered, 'that you told me your own young eyes have seen the sale to slavers, by Lowlanders friendly to the English, of Scottish lads defeated in the Highlands. Believe me, boy: where commerce and tribal rivalry are involved, there are no scruples.'

I reflected there was some rough justice in his words, but was still anxious and be-puzzled. 'Then if,' I asked him, 'there are no obstacles on the land, and none, as you tell me, on the sea, what makes you fear I might not be content upon your vessel?'

The salt eyed me kindly, tho' with some mockery, and thus replied:

'All seafaring, my boy, is hard, brutal and ill-rewarded. Nor would I aver – for I, as I hope you will allow, am neither evil nor hard-hearted – that slavery is much different, in its demands upon a mariner or its effects, from any other kind of seafaring. I have been on whalers, lad, and of the two, would choose a slave-ship. And yet I must confess that, to a young seaman specially, there might seem some difference between harpooning a seal, and any animal more human.' The old salt spat. 'This difference,' he went on, 'is slight; and as one progresses, nurtured by the hard wisdoms of the sea, from the unstable condition of being a ship's boy, to that of becoming a seafarer and a man – and no man is more so than a sailor – this boyish reluctance to ship human flesh will vanish with other immaturities.'

'And I!' I cried. 'Youthful I may be – but shall not I, too, as life instructs me, become such a man as any other?'

'No doubt,' said the salt. 'Yet it remains that you are not so now, whatever you may later come to be.'

I downed the fresh grog he had provided me, and spat, tho' it fell upon my boot. I made to speak, but the Cornishman, restraining me, thus continued:

'I have often reflected on these matters, for as I grow older, I know the dread meeting with my Maker steadily approaches. Yet casting about within my conscience, though I perceive there as we all, being sinners, do, great stains, on the topic of slavery, my spirit reassures me.

'For first, we must consider the nature of these creatures: are they men, as you and I, or are they Hobdignogs?' He paused. 'Nature teaches us to judge of her creatures by their conduct: thus fish acts as fish, fowl as fowl, beast as the beast, and man as human being: whatever their imperfections, their conduct is entire, is typical!' He eyed me candidly. 'In man,' he proceeded, 'even the basest, one may detect our common clay: monsters men may be at times, but utter brutes, unredeemable, I think not. But such, lad, are the slaves: upon them nature has laid a curse that takes from them any savage beauty of the animal, yet bestows on them no potential to glory found in a human creature, even at its most depraved.

'Then, lad, we must reflect upon our Nation: of whom we

are the sons, and to which, in return for its sustaining us, we owe some duty. The commerce of England, and in particular of the West Indies and Americas, which are among the richest treasures of our realm, depends on slavery: remove it, and these jewels vanish! Nay!' he cried, rising and waving his gnarled hand round about him, 'this very city, set above you in its magnificence, would be some lump of cottages were it not for the trade in slaves and sugar that flourishes round about us. There is not one soul, son – not one in this oppulent agglomeration – that is not sustained, in all its civilised pursuits, by the fruits of the cargoes lying about us on these quays!'

He quaffed a larger grog and, fortifying mine, concluded:

'I cannot alas, lad, say to you I am a religious man: too many flecks lie on my conscience to aver it. And yet of the many lessons that the huge seas teach us, is this richest one: that out far upon the deep, beneath its aureole of stars, a man, though but a pin-point in this vastness, may fitly commune there with the Infinite!' He gulped a stalwart dram. 'And so have I, at precious instants of apprehension, alone upon the slaver's heaving bulk, communed.' He shot a gobbet. 'And from the overhanging Universe, there has descended on me, in my questing solitude, a Voice.' He paused and belched a little. 'A Voice compelling, and of infinite reassurance.'

Here the old man, o'ercome with the purity of his emotion, spewed. I helped the good fellow, and restored him to calm with the bottles that a decent wench, employed by the hostelry, brought forward to us in succession. Although, in the North, I had been reared to proper modesty, and to respect for a sex which, though it gave mankind its earliest Temptress, is also that of our dear mothers, my blood, like that of any Scottish lad, was not made of water; nor did the deference I was taught to womankind prevent my natural stirrings in their presence. Yet hitherto, in the more rigorous climate of my native land, I never had clapt eyes on females lavish with their persons as were these Sassenach girls about the inn. With one of them, a maid of I know not quite what count of summers, I soon found myself engaged in a sportive dalliance, spurred in this amiable play by loud encouragements from the good old salt. And when I perceived my hands, aided seemingly – though I am unsure of this in recollection – by the manipulations of the damsel, to be somewhat enmuffled among her skirts and bodices, the worthy Cornishman, raising his beaker, cried out, 'Aye, Jock, we shall make a man out of you yet!'

It was amidst this revelry that there appeared, from out of a bumboat in the harbour, a party of hands that I saw to be from my old ship, the *Providence*, each of them equipped with muskatoons and whips. They joined with us a while in our enlivenment, and told us that they were sent ashore, by Captain Peters, to bring down to the ship the first consignment of the slaves. On hearing this horrid spot to be their destination, my earlier revulsion struck into my heart. But when they called on me to forget past differences, and lend them a comradely hand to perform their duties, the truth came to me that I must no longer hum and haver on this business. And if still doubting somewhat, I recalled two valued precepts given me by my old dominie: the one, that it is better to bite than snarl, and the other, none knows the mount who has not climbed it. So strengthened by this sagacity, and joining my comrades in a final toast, I set off heartily with the slaving party towards the Caves.

The Island

In all human endeavours, as I have been told, and of whatever nature they may be, one half of their success at least lies in the force of habit and routine. Thus it may be in Armies, among soldiers, however fell the slaughters they must perform; and certainly, as I was soon to find, it is in ships. There is so much to do, and constantly; for when no immediate task of navigation is demanded, there remain a hundred essential duties to be carried on; and upon the most junior sailor, many of these are found to fall.

Yet I was not ill used, in the Atlantick, by our crew; or if I was, no more, I have discovered, than is the common lot, on ships, of an apprentice. The petty officers were cruel, the officers blunt and brutal; yet not so wantonly – not even Mr Peters, whose chief torment of me, now he had me safely clapt upon his boat, was that of mockery as much as beatings. As for my fellow seamen, I soon found among them several who were not bullies; and who rather than shouting at me or fetching me a blow, instructed me in their naval arts as best they knew.

For the living cargo in the dungeons of our ship, I felt, if I speak truly, chiefly nothing. Water they must have, and biscuit, and relief from the battened hold into the sea of their frequent and sorry dead. Aside of this – and their consuming stench, and wailings that diminished daily – they were little bother to us. I never even once saw – nor was allowed to for this was the speciality on board of some hardened mariners – the decks along which they lay jamm'd, in dark discomfort, like eels packt in a pie.

I shall not relate, for the adventure is now commonplace, our transit across the ocean as the airs grew warmer. Of our brief dalliance at the Azores, for stores and water, little can be said of note save that two Bristol men, newly signed on, deserted ship there – which had the effect of making those of us remaining who were novices, feel all the more that now we were experienced seamen. In the Doldrums we lingered, and grew quarrelsome, but not long; and were taught to endure the tedium less by patience or even resignation, than by a copious flow of rum: a liquor which, since it emanates from the West Indies, our Captain had plenty of, and cheaply. So busy was I even when my seniors slumbered, about my ship boy's tasks, that I had little time for thinking; which only happened when, between my duties, I snatch'd a moment to look into the volume of John Calvin's texts that was my Uncle's only fair gift to me. These might have fortified my spirit more, had my Latin been any better.

One morning of purest sky, Woad joined me on the hastening prow, and snif't out eagerly at the horizon. 'Two day we theer, man,' he said to me, a smile lighting up his cracked and crafty features.

'You are pleased, Woad, to see your native land again?' quoth I.

'Blood seed, what you tink, then?' he replied and fell to scowling.

'And no doubt,' I pursued, 'you will be seeing your dear Wife and Family once more?'

'Hé, hé, hé,' he uttered, wrenched in mockery. 'He, what

you tink – we slave has wife? No, man, is not permitted. Slave can have nuttin – not even she.'

'Then alas, you are childless, Woad?'

'Hé, he, ho – lissen to this oracle! Child, yes, is much encourage; that like add to the population an' the Planter property. But Mr Planter not know who he daddy is – no, nor not care neither.'

I was surprised. 'But surely, Woad,' I remonstrated, 'even a slave is nurtured by his Owner in the scriptures?'

'Boy, I despair of you,' was all he said.

I did not dispute with the Caribbean, but thought better to take the occasion of asking him more of the swiftly approaching island of St Laughter.

'Well, this is complicate,' said Woad, 'by several factor; but I could put it so. On the island is five chief category of man and woman. First come the Planter: he white, he rich, he drunk, he fornicator: is all, really, you can say about the Planter. Then come the Warrior material: like navy, army, officers and troop: they white, they drunk, they fornicator, but they poor, so they take bribe. Also of course cruel, as they paid to be. Then come Poor Trash: some free, some indenture, some slave like we, but not of course like we. They white, drunk, fornicator, simply evil. Then come black slaves – two classes: labour slave, out in the sugar cane, livin' miseries; and like me, skill slave, which is really the people, as you see, who run the island.'

I laughed at the fellow's merry wit, and asked how Woad and his like, slaves, could in effect run anything.

'Laugh now – see later,' he replied. 'The reason we do is jus' there's no one else to: Planter not bother, sailor and soldier not stay long, white trash too stupid, black slave is chained. That leave we.'

I asked my strange tutor to tell me if he knew anything of
the history of St Laughter; and though I did not doubt him to
be a mine of misinformation, he answered readily enough.
'Well, is like so. First, in the days of innocence, before
Columbo bring on all this trouble, was the Caribes: original
inhabitant, like you is in Scotland, or those passengers we have
below, in Africa. Is not many Caribes left now on St Laughter,
tho' in larger islands I hear is still some kickin' their heels
around.'

'What became, then, of these natives of St Laughter?'

Woad looked round, grinned evilly, and said, 'What you
tink?'

'And were the Dons,' I asked, 'the first white people to
make landfall on the island?'

'Mebbe – but I tink French come there first, cos some old
slave speak patois on the island. English come later on, and
tieve it from the French – that is their custom. But what I
sure of is each of these nation bring out Africans, because
sugar is hard labour, an' it must be cheap.'

'And the principal occupation,' I continued, 'of the island
is cultivation of the cane?'

'Well yes, with fishin' a little and, of course, a bit of . . .
well, that another matter.'

'What is?'

'Ask Mr Varco – he tell you,' Woad answered and, picking
up his cutlass, he made off.

But our preparations for arrival were too scurried for more
enlightenment, and I reflected that reality would soon inform
me of the nature of the island. Even those not on watch rose
far before dawn to spy our landfall, for outlying rocks, some
distance from St Laughter, had already told Mr Peters that

the island now lay just over the circumference. Sure enough, it sheered up in the distance on our port bow, just after the sun; and a cheer rose from the crew that was echoed, in a melancholy manner, by a sort of groan we all heard coming from the hold.

St Laughter is a tropick isle of some eight miles in its greater length, and varying betwixt six and two seen sideways. It has mountains of the smaller sort that are found in Perthshire, but far more precipitous, with some jungle beneath these upper slopes and, as the land flattens to the sea, savannahs now tilled, and given to the cane. There are several small harbours, of which the chief is Campbell Bay (named after none knows whom), on which is situate the main town, or village rather, that is called Joie: a name that may confirm Woad's notion that the island was once ruled by France. The population, which is guessed at more than truly known (for no one has counted it exactly, and there are thought to be escap'd slaves hid in the hills), may be four thousand. The climate is as would be expected: hot, and humid in the rains.

We soon entered into Campbell Bay, and dropt our anchor; whereon we were instantly surrounded by a crowd of craft that put out from the harbour, packed with persons. Many of these tried to clamber up, but were expelled – and even flung back into the sea – on Captain Peters' order, who shouted out, with hearty curses, that we were not ready for their reception.

All morning we worked on opening up the hold: from which there issued, blinking and woebegone, and covered in loathsome slime, the wreckage of our cargo. Most clung together, their shackles clinking, gazing about in liveliest apprehension. Till one tall fellow, whose chain must have snap't off

31

from its neighbour one, leapt suddenly and plunged into the
waves. At this whips were plied on the remainder, to make
them docile – tho' this they were enough, God knows, already; while from the seas below a great shout went up out of
the small boats, which circled round the struggling African,
fighting against his chains' weight, till he gave out a great
scream, the sea reddened, and he was torn beneath by some
Aquatic Monster – much to the rapture of the islanders.

Up on deck, under the Captain's orders, we divided the
Africans into two: those still seeming sturdy were herded into
a huddle on the stern, while others whose limbs were crack'd,
or bore sores specially loathsome, were set aside shivering by
the ship's edge. Here they were slosh'd by us, to render them
less foul, with buckets of sea water; which, though it cleansed
them, made them leap and screech when the salt licked at their
wounds. A ladder was then lowered, and islanders allowed to
board upon payment of a fee – extorted, such was their eagerness and rapacity, at cutlass point. Those admitted now
hurl'd themselves among the weakling slaves, and seized and
handled them exceedingly, like housewives plucking at a
market hen. Sometimes, when two or more purchasers fell
fond of a particular victim, they grabbed onto his limbs as if
they would tear their valued prey asunder. These disputations
our Captain resolved by auction; and in a trice, the hurt
slaves were all disposed of, and carried off by their new
owners down the ladders into the boats, and then away. The
remainder part, which had watched this scene in horror and
consternation, were herded down below again against the sale
of worth-while freight upon the morrow, after they had been
branded and baptised; and in the forenoon, men of more substance were rowed out to us, who gather'd with the Captain

drinking much white rum, and bargaining, I doubt not, about the value of the cargo.

We were not allowed on shore that night, tho' eager enough for it; and much tantalised by the lamps lit on the land, and the far cry of fresh voices, and the dealers in fruits and other favours that came out to us by dark to make trade with the sailors. Such commerce was forbidden us, for our Master feared thieves and, perhaps, desertions; but there was no stopping the seamen, and indeed the petty officers connived at their transactions: the more so as stalwarts bolder and more guileful than the rest, hoisted up some harlots who were shar'd out among the men, upon the poop, in proportion to the seamen's rank, or wealth, or assurance with a cutlass.

Next day, large boats were brought aside, and the small craft chas'd away. In these were stood men with whips, and also soldiers; and along their runnels there lay chains for the slaves' reception. These unfortunates were then usher'd up in Indian file; and with a farewell blow, as if for their good fortune, from the mariners, they were lower'd to the boats and there secured. They were then row'd off, and I never beheld a company more desolate – not even among the emprison'd Highlanders when my father died; and at the thought of this, I wept. But not long, for I was disturbed by a great wail rising from the boats: so methodical a cry, that I took it to be some song, from Africa, in an uncouth language of their own.

After their departure, we younger sailors were made to clear out in the hold; and this took us several days. We worked with our faces muffled, and had often perforce to leap up for air, so violent was the horrid sickness of the atmosphere. There was no light there, save what shot down on us from the open hatch, so that throughout the voyage night must have reigned utterly. The hold was ankle deep in ordure, tinged with red, which we spaded up. And our greatest surprise was how such a multitude could have risen from a place so narrow; remembering, too, that many had died upon the way.

This completed, we made ready for the shore, to which most of the crew had already ventured. I appealed to Mr Peters for some payment for my labours; but got only curses, and the threat that a year's wage at least was due to him for all that he had taught me. I was forlorn at this, for I had dream'd of treats inside the harbour; but I was rescued from my distress by old Varco, who would not go ashore himself, and made me a present of some coins, asking only that I bring him some mangoes from the harbour. So deck'd out in washed gear, I and my young comrades hailed a boat which soon carried us into the island.

Joie is a pretty place: of little streets on slopes, and gay coloured walls with balconies. In the centre, there is a market square smaller than that of Mortar, but since the houses all lie low, seems broader. It has fruit and flower stalls, and some cannon; and the buildings around it are all lit by flares.

But the sailors said our target was called Paradise – a lane further off beside the water, given to rum shops and bordellos. The talk on the ship had all been of the Exploits that the seamen intended on this outing; and they soon set about their preparations by preliminary draughts of rum. The girls were all black, or rather nut-hued; and though they were affable enough, and foreward, I swore I would never lie beside any creature of a cast so utterly repellent. I was much mocked for this by my comrades, who spoke of when in Rome, and such like; to which I replied we were not in Rome, but Joie, and that if they thought the black girls Romans, I saw no Roman males embracing them. At this they laugh'd, and told me a male slave must curb his passion; but for a woman it was different; and called me a Calvinist, making mock of Scotland, which led to fights. In these, I was hit by a rum bottle, and made speechless; and they carried me to a corner, where the women put some poultices, and made me easy.

The Orchard

WE STAYED for some weeks in Joie, loading molasses; and there was little labour for the crew, for we had slaves to do it. This gave us the joy of those who, thinking themselves slaves on board, found there were others that were really so. And feeling ourselves Masters, as in truth we were, we kept the slaves at it without let or pity.

I had decided the ship should sail without me. I had no hankering to be a sailor, no love for Peters, and an honest desire for wages for my work. This island might not be Eden, but it should offer me better prospect of advancement than a slaver. Fearing that if he knew of my intent, Peters might kidnap me away, I kept silent lest word come to him of my desire; only unfolding my secret to old Varco, whom, since he was a Celt, I trusted.

He thought my prospects on St Laughter not to be brilliant, unless I enlisted as a tar or soldier, which would be a harsher discipline than that I purposed to escape from. On the plantations, there could be nothing for me: for everything there was lord or slave, with no place in between. Perhaps among the poor free whites I might find some employment; though many of these, he said, were near to be slaves themselves. But he gave me the name of a Mr Trenoggin, a fellow countryman, who, he said, conducted a small orchard that supplied English fruits to the officers and planters; the which, being rare upon the island and thus prized, came costly, and made Mr Trenoggin a decent livelihood.

I called accordingly upon Trenoggin, whom I found, after enquiry, to inhabit a ramshackle house, or rather hutment, some quarter mile out of Joie. In the fields around it, I saw a few slaves carrying water to the fruit trees; and as I approached the dwelling, there was a great cackling of lean dogs. The door was opened by a young slave of my own age, who had the effrontery to grin at me, and ask in a pert voice, 'Wassa want now, my young mistah?'

'Conduct me instanter,' I ordered, 'to the presence of you Master.'

'Hop in, man,' he answered, bowing me through the door, and waving like some Courtier to the dank room beyond. From this there came snores and fartings; and as my eyes grew habituated to the hot gloom, I perceived spread-eagled on a slattern couch, or mattress, an elderly fellow somewhat bloated, hectic and unshaven. 'Meet the boss,' said the slave with a grimace.

'What is your name, fellow?' I asked the lad severely.

'Is Archibald,' he answered. 'What you call?'

I deigned not to answer but, slapping my knife against my thigh, said, 'Who else is there, Archibald, beside Mr Trenoggin, in the household?'

'You mean like slave?' he answered. 'Well, first is me – I like Mr Trenoggin pet. In the kitchen is Priscilla, who do cook an' ting. Hey, come out here me darlin',' he yelled high-pitched through a curtained door.

A bright girl appeared, of perhaps some fourteen summers, holding a bleeding hen and a knife that flashed reflections to her eyes. 'This here Priscilla,' Archibald explained. 'Back to your kitchen, woman, and behave yourself.'

'Go – way,' she replied, and pounced out briskly.

'Then in the orchard,' Archibald continued, 'is like two

more: is Daniel, he the wise man and our eldest; then is Alfonso, he like wilder, see, not a tranquil boy like me.'

'And Mr Trenoggin,' said I, indicating my recumbent host. 'Will he awake soon, do you imagine?'

'Oh, is no problem,' Archibald replied, and much to my astonishment, he tumbled his Master out onto the floor, with a thump like an oatmeal sack, then poured water from an earth pot violently on his person.

The Cornishman awoke, looked round him in blear puzzlement then, spotting Archibald, called feebly for rum. This the slave brought him and, after an eager gurgle, he perceived me at last, and asked me how I did.

I told him well, and said that I brought him the greetings of his compatriot, Mr Varco.

'Ah, how is the old pirate?' my host enquired.

'Pirate, sir? You jest!' cried I.

'Not so,' said Trenoggin, gobbling down a rum. 'For he and I, you see, in our younger days, served under good Captain Ventry, a minor buccaneer in the West Indies, but superb.'

'Is piracy, sir, then rife around the islands?'

'God's teeth it is!' the old reprobate replied. 'Betwixt sugar and piracy, if it comes to profit, there is not much to choose in Caribbean waters.' He sighed, and slung a slog. 'But alas,' he continued, 'just as the big planters encroach upon the smaller, so do the larger fleets eat up more moderate flotillas. Today, in these oceans, one may say that only galleys led by Nayle, Gasshe, and Orrifus are of much importance – gallant seamen though these Captains be.'

'But sir!' I cried. 'Surely this evil is suppress'd by the authorities?'

Trenoggin gave me a huge guileful wink. 'Suppression, as the poet has it, more honoured in the breach than in the gallows. For consider, lad. If our pirate ships assail the French and Spaniards, and bring up goods and slaves inside our ports, who are our Governors to complain of this? And what is more . . .' he gave me a great leer '. . . might not our rulers participate, financially as it were, in these profitable and clandestine forays?'

'May one then, Mr Trenoggin, avow openly a piratical connection?'

'Nay, lad,' cried the aboriculturalist, growing grave. 'A small pirate, such as myself – and even one who is so no longer – must speak prudently; and in this, my boy, I depend on your discretion. But as for men like Nayle, Gasshe and Orrifus, they may sail freely where they will; and indeed, Captain Gasshe was even made Governor in a colony for some years.'

I was much astounded by this intelligence till, remembering my purpose, I told him of my hope of settling in St Laughter. The late pirate listened carefully then, after a reflective rum, thus spoke:

'You must first make sure,' he said, 'that Peters has no wind of your intention; and for this, you should slip ashore at the last moment possible before he sails, for otherwise he will send searching for you, and on this island every face is known. As for an occupation, I must be open with you. The purchase of my small plot, the trees, this hovel and the four slaves who serve me, eat up my small piratical accumulations; and from the sale of fruits, the income barely sustains my household and my grog. But for good old Varco's sake, and because you are Celtic and a likely lad, I could take you on as a worker in return for nourishment. Then, with Peters sailed, and you established more secure in Joie, you could look around, if you so wished, for better.'

'And could you hide me, sir, until the slaver's far departed?'

'On that I must reflect,' the old Cornishman replied. 'For under the ship's articles, that I doubt not Peters has well forged, for me to take you would be to harbour a deserter, to wit a crime fit for the lashing-block and shackles.'

I had perforce to be content with this and, thanking the old rogue, said I would not trouble him again until the ship was two days out from land; and that how I would contrive to remain hid during the interim, must be left to my own courage and resource. He congratulated me on my enterprise, grasped my hand warmly, and offered me a lurching toast; sending meanwhile Archibald around the orchard to fetch some fruits for me to carry to his old comrade Varco on the ship.

So I bade him farewell and, carrying these, set off downhill towards Joie, where I could see lying below in the harbour our little vessel like a dot upon a pearl. Whereat I heard a clink and patter, and was overtook by Archibald, who seized my arm; and said to me he had overheard my parley with his Master (about being hid), and would offer me a hiding-place, upon conditions.

'Lissen now, Mistah Man,' said he. 'If you slip off the ship, see, and trot up here, prudent like, me an' the boys will hustle you up into the hills behind the orchard, and bring you food an' ting until you safe to reappear.'

'And your conditions, Archibald?'

He gleamed at me. 'I want that knife,' said he, 'or one jus' like it.'

'Surely,' I remonstrated, 'a slave may not possess a weapon?'

'Sure he may not!' Archibald replied.

'But can you move up with me to the hills without discovery?'

'To the hills yes: but not down into Joie where, if we get catch that far from the orchard, we get lash.'

'Very well,' I said. 'When I hear of our sailing day, I shall try to let you know in time.'

'An' the knife?' asked Archibald, eyeing it tenderly.

'Will be yours,' I said.

'Tank you,' said he.

The Hill

WHEN the molasses were all loaded on, and fresh food and water, and no crew allowed on shore that night, I knew our departure would be in the morning, though Captain Peters had not told us so. But a loud party in the poop for the planters that had bought his slaves, with toasts, choruses, and good loyal huzzahs, assured me that farewells were being taken.

My problem was how to get ashore, and I had long brooded on it. By his keen eye, I knew that Varco guessed at my intent; but I dare not speak to him about it lest he perchance betray me, or be forced by Peters' blows, once my slipping off was noticed, to reveal his secret. From our anchorage to the shallows was some twenty chain; and I still could not swim, and besides I feared the shark and barracuda. To steal a boat would be convenient, but all the small craft now lay beside the mole at nightfall. Perhaps my best hope was to climb aboard the boats sent out to fetch the Captain's guests. But they carried lanthorns, and there would be many on board observing my departure.

When these boats had come out from the shore, and tied up alongside, they were ordered to wait the pleasure of their Masters, carousing in the poop. And after a cautious while I climbed down the ladder to see if I could parley with their crews, and so deceive them. There were chained slaves resting at the oars, and two white sailors to each boat, with pistols. To them I asked, by way of making inter-course, if there was anything on the ship they needed, and I could get them which they would trade with me for their rum.

At this they laugh'd, saying they well understood a sailor's lust for spirits, but what could a poor young seaman offer them in return for it? Till one, a coxcomb whose mother, to judge by his dark hue, had known carnal commerce with the slaves, said what he might wish for was a pair of those bell-bottoms that the Navy have, and which he had seen some of our older sailors, that had served in men-of-war, still wore to seem more glorious. For a pair of these, he said, untatter'd, a jar of rum would be mine for the asking.

This caused me some perplexity: for only the older and more violent of our crew possessed this garment, which they treasur'd as a peacock does its tail; but then I remembered one of our Quartermasters that had them, and how on the voyage he has made some ill Proposals to me, by which I believed I might now benefit.

I therefore climbed up again and sought out this fellow, whom I found slumbering upon his watch; and wakening him up gently, I asked him if he could give me some tobacco; letting my hands stray a little, as if wantonly, when he handed me a ration for my pipe. I lit it and thanked him with a coy-ness in my eye, and sweet admiration in my speech, such as made me seem to him some Queen of Sheba, rapt beside her Solomon in his glory.

At this tone of mine the Quartermaster, grunting and muttering thickly, clap't his sweaty arms about me, in a clutch like an orang-outang. But tho' almost squeez'd of breath by his endeavours, I insinuated to him that tho' 'twas true his purposes could be achieved after some fashion with his bell-bottoms still about him, should he remove these, the play of his limbs would be freer and more lusty. At this he unclip't me, and with a roar of anticipatory glee, tore off the garment and swung round upon me once again; but I, leaping up like a gazelle, snatch'd away his nether clothing, and darted off among the forests of the rigging; where, tho' he pursued me bellowing about the ship, I easily eluded him, and slipt down to the bumboat with my prize.

This the young Mulatto seized from me with ecstasy, and was honest in his own part of the bargain. Whereon I, assuming a generous credulity, offered my rum around the boats; and when they were made merry, I began heaving sighs like a tornado. They asked what ailed me, and I said that on the shore, in Joie, I had left all of my heart with a slave-girl called Priscilla; and that if I could not see her once more before we sailed, I knew that I would die of anguish.

They laugh't at this, and slapp'd my shoulder, and shared with me some more rum. But my grief seemed not abated, till at last, falling on my knees and clutching my hands together, I besought them to hide me in the furl'd sails of the boat, and carry me secretly ashore. I would lie quiet, I promised them, till their passengers were disembarked; and as for the return journey, I knew a boat of ours was coming in the morning to pick up our seamen landed with a fever; and that in this, I would come back upon our vessel.

They debated at length on my petition, dubious and in dispute, till at last the Mulatto, who was softer-hearted than his comrades (and also I think drunker), said he would hide me as I wished; but that if I was discovered I must say I had swum into their boat myself, and hidden secretly in the sails without their knowledge; and to this they all at last agreed, and hid me.

At length, the slavers came tumbling down the ladder, making the boat lurch as they stumbled in; and after shrill yells and laughter (the harsh voice of Peters making me quake amid the damp folds of the sails), the whips were laid on the slaves' backs, and we row'd off. Their singing drowned the soft plash of the oars; and before an hour, we had grounded by the mole, where I waited anxious till all the voices had receded.

Then I crep't out, and circled Joie along the beach, meaning to turn inland when I should guess myself opposite Mr Trenoggin's orchard. In Joie, all was still with stars; and there was only the splash of waves upon the lava, and suck as they fell back. Onward I clambered over juts, stopping each minute to catch my heart-beat. Till a red crack split, my neck snapp'd, and a cry shot, 'Slave out!'

Soldiers pursued me, firing, and I clutched a hand to my flowing shoulder. Best to evade them, I waded out, till my head was one lump among those around of coral, and my skin lanced with the salt pain. They ran shouting to and fro, but did not think about the sea. I waited, still trembling.

But then was another fright: for round my leg, there whipp'd the fangs, with knife sting, of some Sea Horror; I let out a dull cry, and lurch'd back up the wet sand, struggling; where I fell exhausted, bleeding at both ends.

There I remained till the stars faded, weakened and fearful and alone; till with a prayer to St Andrew, and my dear Father's memory, I stagger'd up and stole into the outer streets of Joie, creeping round towards the country. Asses brayed now, and dogs cried distantly; but I saw no human till I reached the track up to the orchard.

Behind the hutment, and at a distance, I had noticed a shed, or lean-to of palms, where I divined the slaves would all be housed; and stealing up to this, I called out in a low voice, 'Archibald!' There was a stirring from a snore, and the face of the blackamoor peep'd out through the fronds. 'Blood seed,' the lad whispered, 'is the Buckra boy. Come in our yard, man, and meet the company.'

I stole within, and found two others rising from the soil, and rubbing eyes. The short, heavy-bearded slave was Daniel, who gave me a hard glance but said nothing to me, and fell to prayer. The other, Alfonso, was a tall lean fellow, imposing if there be any choice of beauty in their ugliness. He greeted me with a smile I trusted not, and said, 'Hé, look like ole Mr Barracoot been eatin' you.'

Archibald patch'd my bleedings which, though their pain was exquisite, came from shallow wounds; and gave me a horrid root called, he said, akee, and water which was their morning fare. I asked where Priscilla lodged, and got a leer. 'Where you tink, man?' he said, waving his hand toward the hut of old Trenoggin. 'Come we go hurry now, or that woman she come out to peep and pry.'

I set off with Archibald towards the hills; and the land past the orchard soon grew steep and rugged, with trees and dank bushes, thickening around. Archibald, hastening on despite his chains, kept stopping angrily while I clambered up. I told him he forgot I had lost blood, nor walked on dry land for weeks; but he only cried, 'Blood clot – go way now,' which I understood not.

At last we reached a shelf of rock, with shrub overhanging,

where he stopp'd. 'This 'ere your Eden garden,' the slave told
me, 'jus' you wait ear till the boat go – you can see she sailing,'
and he pointed out towards the bay.

'And you will bring food to me, Archibald?'

'Me try, man. But is breadfruit, mango and nut for you,
and water, if you creep down a bit and hunt for them, you
see?' He smiled hard at me. 'An' now what you do, is give that
knife to me like you say.'

I unsheathed and handed it to him and he shot a glance at it
and clap't it fast to my throat. 'So now you die, boy,' he
whispered, with his white teeth in the dawn light.

God be praised that in danger, we need not rely on our poor
wits, but leave the action to that instinctive part which, though
casket for our souls, is animal. The slave's hands were free,
piercing the dagger at my neck, the other clutching on my
hair; but his feet were still shackled, so I lay back quick, tug-
ging my hair out of his grasp, and kicked out at his knees so
that as he tottered back he stumbled, the knife flying from his
claw over the precipice. I started up, and seizing the chain
despite his kicks, dragg'd him round about the shelf till his
head beat on the rocks, he crying out for mercy. So letting go,
and holding a sharp rock, I stood above him.

'Oh well,' he said, 'was like a mistake, you know, man.'

'Murderer!' cried I.

'No, man, no, I would not say so. Put down that stone,
now, and let we have a little piece of conversation.'

Amazed by his effrontery, and pleased with the success of
my manoeuvre, I could not feel harshly to him, though I was
still vigilant. 'Why did you do it?' I cried angrily.

'Well, you see,' said Archibald, 'I make you a confession.
Is like me, and Daniel, and Alfonso who you meet, we plan

one day to take off to the hills, and for this your knife would be so beautiful.'

'But I offered you the weapon!'

'Yes man, I know. But later on, you would not keep quiet about it: you shoot your mouf so loud that you betray we.'

'True,' I allowed.

'But yes, man, of course you would – and you will now. All Bukra must betray promise to a slave.'

'But how can we ever trust you?'

'Right! Never at arl, man – would upset the system. But jus' now – please tink a little. Is you got to trust we, I believe.'

'After your treachery?'

'Man, is quite simple. You could kill me, yes, but then Daniel and Alfonso know where I go, and Mr Trenoggin not like you slay his property. But if you let me go, how you know I not tell down there is a deserter hidden in the hill?'

I saw that the slave, tho' a savage, possessed some powers of reasoning. Nor, now that my life was sav'd, and he harmless, could I wish him much further ill. I therefore hoisted him to his feet, and told him to make off, and that if he betray'd me I would denounce his attempted murder, and he would hang. He made no reply (save for a smile) and after hunting a while, out of my reach and vainly, for the knife, he clanked off down the hill and was soon lost to view.

During the morning, I watched our ship sail: I thought there was some flurry up on deck, and saw a boat lower'd, come into port, and make out back again. But soon the sails hung and billowed, and the *Providence* set out for its voyage home. And tho' I was relieved to see it go, I shed tears to think it was headed toward Scotland, and I now committed, alone and powerless, to this tropick wilderness.

In the afternoon, rain fell in great gushes, and I grew chill and hungry; and by nightfall, I decided I could wait no longer before disclosing myself to Mr Trenoggin. So I clambere'd down, and tho' descending, found the way harder than when coming up, for the jungle was matted, and I knew not the tracks. Lost and exhausted, I came to the fields a mile off from the orchard; and made my way wearily towards Trenoggin's hut.

He seemed surprised to see me, and I guessed he had not believed that I would persevere with my intent – I mean of staying on the island. But he received me well enough, and got me food, and some dry clothing. Tomorrow, he said, he would show to me my duties, which would be chiefly to drive the donkey cart to deliver fruit to the garrisons and plantations. He added slyly I would not need to take money from his customers, for everything would be done by bills, which he would himself collect.

He said he was going out to Joie, to visit rum shops, and how he would listen to any rumour of desertion, and find if there was any danger to me. Before he went off, he poured me a dram and, turning severe, addressed me in this manner:

'You know, boy, that in this house there is a female slave, Priscilla. Perhaps you may think that for a white man to lie with a savage is a disgrace; or if you do not think this, that a young man's lust has rights above an older man's greater worth.' At this he snarled evilly, but like a clown. 'Let us have no mistake, misunderstanding,' he continued. 'I own Priscilla, and not you; and if I discover you have laid as little as a traitor finger on her, I shall see, lad, I promise you, that the Navy's press-gang will hear much of you.' Here he poked a gnarl'd finger on my knee. 'Do not imagine, either,' he went on, 'that even if you can hide secrets from me, I shall not know how to whip them out of the bitch.' Here he toasted me, more cheerfully. 'Just be patient, lad,' he said, 'and sensible; for once you are settled safely in, we shall soon find some black slut for your satisfaction; and if you work hard, and prosper, you can buy one of your own.' I hotly denied his insinuation, telling him that besides the debt of gratitude I owed him, the aspect of the slaves was odious to me. At this he clapp'd me on the back (causing my wound to ache), and staggered off into the evening.

He had hardly made off along the track to Joie, sitting lurching astride the donkey's arse (whose name was Comely), when Priscilla peep'd inside, and came to do some tidying that was not, in truth, much needed. She did not speak to me at all, that is with her lips, but her bright eyes did so, and also, so to say, her rump and bosom, and indeed each part of her.

'Tell me, Priscilla,' I said to her, keeping that distance to my voice that I deemed proper. 'The slaves Daniel and Alfonso: they are good lads like Archibald?'

'Hé, hé – you make joke?' she cried. 'Is *bad* boys, each one of them, I tell you.'

'And why, girl, do you say this?'

She sat down unbidden on Mr Trenoggin's frowsty couch, bit her lips prettily and frown'd, then said to me, 'Well, Archibald, he is like sly, you know; an' Alfonso, he like violent; an' Daniel, he the worst of all – he act holy, but is hypocrip.'

'So only you, Priscilla,' I said smiling, 'have any virtue here among the slaves?'

'Me?' she said, rising. 'No, I bad girl too: very bad – you see!' And she flounc'd out so prettily that tired tho' I was, and repelled by her unnatural hue, I was dismayed to feel my blood rising; but feeling my aches and wounds, and remembering my promise to Trenoggin, I lay down on some rotten pillows, in the corner, and soon slumbered.

The Plantation

As DAY passed after day, on this island where all seemed timeless, I became an accepted face upon St Laughter. Everyone knew, or soon discovered, that I had escaped from the slave ship; but tho' this was a crime, it was not held much against me, when they saw my youth and learned how I had been almost press'd on board at Bristol. Had Peters been there to bring an accusation, I have no doubt they would have punished me cruelly; but with no one to prosecute, and I seeming a useful, polite and inoffensive lad, they let me be; tho' some liked to tease me with threats of jail, and bastinadoes.

Driving the donkey-cart, I learned my way about the island; or at any rate, that part of it nearest in to Joie. And because those who could afford the rare fruits of Trenoggin were mostly men and women of some substance, I had a glimpse – though through servants' doors and gossip – of how the island aristocracy, as I might call it, managed their affairs. And before I relate the sudden shattering to my fortunes, I shall describe, for those who may have any interests in the West Indies, how the economy of this small island was conducted.

St Laughter has no Governor: for it is the smallest of a chain of islands that are ruled jointly by the viceroy to His Majesty whose palace is on the largest, called Resurrection. From time to time, they said in Joie, the Governor takes ship and makes a procession round the smaller islands of his king-

dom; but often a year or more may pass before this Potentate
sets foot in Joie.

St Laughter, then, is like a kingdom without a monarch:
his authority is present, but not he. This means that all those
holding power of any kind use it in his name; making a score
of tyrants where, on Resurrection, there is but one.

The hierarchy, or pyramid of power upon the island, is
much as Woad had told me earlier. The Planters and Officers
are rival barons, despising each other, yet allied against the
rest. The poor whites are jealous, quarrelsome and treacherous; and I had little dealings with them, if I could. The white
slaves are miserable, and the black ones beyond misery. But
some slaves of both races that have skills, or cleverly corrupted
masters, achieve a precarious independence that one accident,
or false gesture on their part, can utterly destroy; so that they
tumble to greater horrors than those they rose from.

To see slavery, it does not suffice to know domestic slaves
in Joie, oppress'd and restricted tho' their lives may be. To
learn of their full condition, and indeed the object of the slave
oeconomy, a Plantation must be visited, and I knew many. In
St Laughter, these are smaller than in other places, since the
island itself is small; and all slaves agree, so Archibald assured
me, that the larger the colony of serfs, the worse. Though
how anything could be wretcheder than Valentine, I can not
conceive.

Valentine, tho' not the largest estate of Laughter, is the
nearest big one to the capital. Its owner, Mr Wilson, lives in
England, where he sits in the House of Commons for a
southern borough, and comes only to the Caribbean when his
profits seem to slacken. He is unencumbered much by any
family, since his wife is long dead, and his sons, I heard, are in

the Americas, or on larger islands. Of his flesh in Valentine there are none save a few old Aunts, that even the white overseers call rooks, who sit squawking and pecking about the verandahs of the plantation house.

Of slaves, Valentine has two hundred: twenty domestic, and the rest out in the fields. These are controlled, in chief, by Mr George, a Welshman, aided by some poor whites, and despotick blacks. In overseers, the slaves prefer a drunkard: for though he is brutal, he has no method in his cruelty. But Mr George, a Dissenter, does not drink, and executes cold justice.

The slaves toil while there is light, then sleep. There is no rest in daytime, and only short moments for water and the needs of nature, so that they become Machines. The lash is not used so much for punishment – tho' this occurs – as for a constant goad, like a jockey wields his whip. And indeed, when the overseers lay on the lash there is little passion, it is but Automatick. Sometimes the slaves sing, tho' dolefully; and this is not prohibited for, like our shanties, it eases toil.

The only protection of a plantation slave lies in his value: the money he cost, and that his toil will earn; so tho' a Planter will think nothing of slaying a slave that might defy him, he will prefer to lash him this side of the point of death. There are but few self-murders, I was told; so brutal are the dim minds of the slaves, or perhaps obstinate.

Their only enjoyment is such carnal knowledge of the female slaves as is allowed them; and this is regulated not according to their needs but to their Masters', for procreation by them of slave children. The only safeguard of the women – though it is but little – is that no man should approach them that the overseer does not deem fit to give them robust children. But the crews of lean half-caste scavengers about the house show'd well enough the overseer was disobey'd, or connived at commerce with ill-favoured whites.

For a black slave carnally to approach a white – even herself a slave – is rewarded by the lash and death. This is, indeed, in Laughter, the only utter crime and ignominy. Lewd fellows told me that loose white women (and indeed, some more dainty) torture the blacks by forcing their embraces with the threat of crying rape; and when the blacks yield in fear to them, cry rape all the same; but this I can hardly credit, if only because the black slaves, tho' robust, are so horrid.

The rules of this oeconomy are well understood by all; for the threat of pain and death sharpens the understanding even of the simplest or most wilful. But each time a slaver puts into port, there is something of an Eruption; for to the slaves fresh from Africa, this society is new, and has to be learned fast by pain.

Thus, at Valentine, I observed the induction of Africans that we had brought there. These brutes, bewildered and terrified, could scarcely grasp what was required of them; the more so as their crude speech was alien, and a whip the only tongue. Their instruction was left by Mr George and his fellows chiefly to the blacks rear'd in St Laughter; who, forgetting their own ancestry, shew'd the Africans no pity. Tho' perhaps, as the Hottentots grew familiar with the island climate, and learned its ways, there was a growing commerce between them and the slaves born in the Caribbean.

I was soon to learn more nearly about a slave's condition; but at that first sight of it, tho' I did not admire all that I saw, I felt no profound revulsion. My nation and countrymen told me this was right; and so did the faith that Knox, of blessed memory, imparted to us Scots, at any rate in the Lowland part: namely, that man's fate, on earth and even beyond it, is preordained at birth. Nor can I deny that, since my own state on the island was precarious, to see others in a condition more so, gave me a sort of consolation; for it meant that those in authority searching for delinquents, would cast their eyes on others before me.

Even so, I had some doubts, which I attributed less to a sick conscience than to my youth. And perhaps it was to resolve these, feeble though they were, that I had recourse to Mr George, when I found that the overseer, seeing me often at the plantation, took a sort of fancy to me. For he would lead me to his hut and give me fruits from the basket I had sold him; and ask me about Scotland, which I think he esteemed a sort of barbaric Wales, tho' superior as well to England.

Mr George was a short barrel'd man of great power of limb and character. His eyes were frank, and star'd out hard at you; but whether this was the openness of honesty or cruelty, I was not sure. My first big surprise, when knowing him better I embark'd upon the question of the slaves, and their condition, was that he deemed my theology of the matter so much rubbish.

'John Knox,' he said, 'was a spry article, true enough. But his doctrine of predestination was designed to prove that he was predestined to rule Scotland. But we here do not need such pretexts for our power. For their justification lies simply in the fact that it exists.'

'But so bleak a belief, Mr George,' I said, 'can lend authority to any tyranny.'

'Yes indeed,' he cried jovially. 'I command slaves by the

whip, and I allow it; and had he my whip and, even more, my gun, I would expect him to try to command me, and I fight him for it.'

'Then your rebuke to the Africans, sir, is that they did not fight?'

'Oh, I have no doubt they did! For after all, when they fight among themselves – as they often do before we catch and flog them – they can all battle well enough. But the only fact of any consequence is that when they fought us, they lost.'

'But mayhap, sir, they had handicaps: I mean with numbers, and with weapons.'

Here he laughed loud. 'Life takes no account of handicaps, boy!' cried he. 'If I fight you – nay, have no fear! – 'twill be to kill you, or you me; and I shall not reproach you for trying to take my life if I mean to take yours away.'

'But you and I, sir, are not savages!' I cried. 'And surely you do not admit that inferior beings like the slaves have the same right to our lives as we to theirs?'

'Who says they are savages?' cried Mr George, with a great bellow. 'Believe me, and I know them, they can think and feel as well as you and I. They may not know Latin, or how to handle a muskatoon; but they could learn both, depend upon it, if they wished. And as to that,' he continued, poking me in the rib, 'can you speak their tongue, or use their assegais?'

'Then Mr George: there is no difference? None at all?'

'None, lad, that I can see: save that here in Laughter, we are up and they are down; and in those two postures it is entirely to our interest, yours and mine, that both races should remain.' He laughed again, and handed me a plum. 'Now, do not look shock'd, lad,' he said, 'and do not feel . . .' here he looked dark at me '. . . you have to tell each fool upon the island what I say. But let me assure you, boy: that if I am the best overseer on the island, I mean who wrings the top figure for our sugar, it is because I know that our sole and only object here is to grind the last guinea out of the sugar and the slaves.'

The Welshman's view was rare upon the island, for most, I discover'd, thought nothing at all about the slaves – I mean, considered them to be an element of nature, like the sky; while others, especially among the poor whites, had theories about them that, the more I thought of Mr George's words, seemed to me fantastickal; as indeed any theory must be which puts God and Nature invariably on the side of any man's own advantage. As to the slaves themselves, those who would speak out at all agreed heartily with the whites that they were inferior beings; as I suppose I would too, if a wrong answer should earn me a hundred lashes.

But prudent as our farm slaves were at Mr Trenoggin's, with all answers to my questions clearly loaded with deceit, a greater familiarity, and a certain relaxation on the orchard (due most to the Cornishman's great love of the rum bottle), made them speak sometimes, even in my presence, a little perhaps as they spoke among themselves. And I surmised this part of frankness was also due to my being their own age (indeed, younger than Daniel and Alfonso), and, though a white, one they knew well to be a person of no substance on the island, and not born there.

Of this trio – for Priscilla was too young and flighty (besides being a girl) for any serious intercourse – the most grave, and yet ambiguous, was Daniel. In conversation, which he never would begin unless I did, he sought to trick me with a kind of duplicity that consisted in his claiming access to God; and then carrying the argument into a realm of theology where, if I were true to my beliefs, he could seek to put me at a disadvantage. Often he vexed me so, that I would conquer the argument by reminding him he was a slave; whereat he would fall silent, and not speak to me again for days, until I seemed to repent, and almost pleaded.

Daniel's God (so I was told by Archibald) was of a kind worshipp'd in a faith called *obeah*; and has, so far as I could grasp, a sort of pagan deity that, carried over first with the slaves from Africa, has been transformed by the black islanders into the fount of a demonic cult. This god spoke only to black ears; and to propitiate it, and win its gifts, a sort of witchcraft of blood and bones and magick incantations was demanded. It could bless, and it could curse; and for him who believed in it, it could do either. All the slaves, said Archibald, were its rapt adherents; and whites too, tho' they denied it.

I taxed Daniel with this fell superstition, since I knew he was familiar with the rudiments of the Christian faith and was, at any rate, a fine singer of our hymns. He first refused to say a word, save to express deep annoyance that Archibald had told me anything; but when I persisted (for my interest was to wean his black soul from the damnation hovering over it), he consented to discuss this doctrine with me; tho' warning me, with a loftiness I confess greatly annoyed me, that even what little part he could explain, I would be unable at all to understand.

My discourse with Mr George on slave conditions had made me decide that the doctrine of predestination was not the one I would hammer off with; so I began in more general

59

Christian terms, by telling him the chief proofs of our faith to be: the revelations of our Lord, the example of the Saints, and Miracles.

'An' with *obeah* is similar,' he answered glumly.

'But how can that be?' I said, meaning to chide the fellow towards Truth.

'The Lord of we reveal heself like *demon*, like *strong demon*,' he said pleasantly. 'An' he reveal heself personal to *me*.'

I shook my head, smiling. 'Hé, boy!' he asked me. 'That Lord of yours – you *see* him ever?'

'Not I, but the Disciples,' I rejoined.

'Dead men!' he answered. 'Our Lord, he appear to me like *there*.' He pointed, and my head darted around.

'Appear to we *Saint*,' he continued. 'We got saint too, boy, and we saint *livin*'.'

'But what,' I asked him, 'is the proof of this?'

'We prove it like you, with miracle. Hé, you like to see a miracle, maybe?'

I smiled indulgently.

'Well, boy, I offer you a couple. Wait!' Daniel shut his eyes, and sat for a while in a vibration. Then he said, 'Trenoggin die, Priscilla she make baby.'

At this I laugh'd. 'It needs no miracle,' I said 'to know that Mr Trenoggin will not live forever, nor Priscilla cling rigorously to her chastity.'

'Peace and love,' said Daniel, and would speak no more. So seeing the fellow was too ignorant and deprav'd for my ministrations, I departed.

For now I must carry a huge load of sweet potatoes into Joie, for the military there, so I called Alfonso from the fields that he should load them. The lad resented my command; for

Alfonso had a sickly pride, and I saw 'twas an error to be indulgent to the slaves, for they sought to take advantage of my youth. Vex'd with Alfonso, I ordered him to run beside me while I drove the donkey-cart, which he did, his chains clanking viciously along the rocks.

The regiment in Joie was from North England, I believe Lincolnshire; tho' the officers were chiefly London men. The soldiers were country matter, ignorant and uncouth; and it often amaz'd me how, tho' a year now in St Laughter, they knew nought of it save for taverns, while of the country round about, learned only by slave-hunting in the hills. When I had asked one of them, a Corporal, what next settlement his regiment might go to, he told me to Madras; and I found that, centuries after Columbus, the fellow believed India lay just beyond Campbell Bay.

It was imprudent to bring Alfonso too far in, for if the troops treated me with no more than disdain, to slaves they were most cruel; buffeting them, and forcing them at bayonet-point to tasks about the barracks which, when they came home late, caused their Masters to rebuke and beat them for delay. So when Alfonso had unloaded the potatoes, I told him to remain steady in the yard, while I would carry the cargo into the encampment.

In the Lines, the troops were relaxing from their guard, cleaning their kits and buttons, and chattering like crows in all those blasphemies and banalities that are their staple. Till one of them, a great loon called Drummer Guelphe, who lov'd to mock, seized hold of me and said that I must join them in a toast. I accepted well enough, and took their glass; but then Guelphe said the toast was 'Death and Confusion to the Pretender and the Scots rebels'.

'Come, Jock,' cried he. 'We know you are one of the good North Britons, and a Hanoverian to boot.'

True I was no lover of Charles Edward, nor of the Romish superstitions of my Father's tribe; yet what Scottish lad could not feel wonder, and some admiration, at the Highlanders' invasion into Derby, or the dismay they struck into proud English hearts? Besides, after Culloden, I had seen the fruits of their revenge, and the barbarities of Stinking Billy and his Hessians. So this was a toast, if Scots had proposed it, I might have swallowed; but not if ordered to me by a malignant Sassenach.

'I shall pledge you a more honest toast, Drummer Guelphe,' I cried. 'And that is, to King George, and the Union of our peoples.'

'Nay, Jock!' cried Guelphe, seizing the rum glass and forcing it to my lips. 'Death and Dismay to the rebels of the White Rose.'

Some soldiers called out to leave me be, one crying, in their English style, 'What the fucking fuck it matter so long as 'e fucking drinks?' But Guelphe, spur'd to mulishness by this challenge to his authority, grabbed me by the neck to crack my teeth open with the glass. Whereat I laid a foul kick into his gut so, with a yell, he loos'd me; and some held back the Drummer (bent now on murder), while others spurr'd me on humorously to renewed attack. When into this clamour and confusion there strode the Lieutenant of the Watch whose name, I knew, was Johnstone, and he a Lowlander.

At this there fell silence, save for the click of heels; and in grovelling tones that should have shamed a veteran, Guelphe named me as a pesty rebel who, he swore violently, had 'called for a toast to the King across the Water'; and no soldier spoke up for me to deny this lie.

This Johnstone listened quietly, with cold eyes; then silenced the Drummer, and turned their glare onto me. He asked me my name, and who my father was, and cousins, and from which clan and glens in Scotland, nodding and saying nothing to my answers. Then he examined his troops concerning me, and they gave ready answers, little to my favour. To all this he listened carefully, showing no sign, but sometimes darting me a look. Then he turned on his heel, saying only to them, 'Get rid of him,' with no more concern than if I was a dog.

They pulled off their belts, and lash'd me merrily into the courtyard, I running towards our cart. But here they found merrier play to torture our poor slave, and their favourite trick was to stoop fast and catch Alfonso by his fetter, spinning him over till his head crack'd like a melon on the stones. They climbed on the cart, and raced the donkey round the yard, whipping it to a braying frenzy; and when I, or Alfonso, tried to seize it back, they hurl'd potatoes at us like a cannonade. There was nought we could do but escape without our cart, and our bones still mercifully unbroken.

Along the road out to the orchard, Alfonso said not a word, nor would he answer when I spoke to him, or even let me try to stay his bleeding. And such a fury was he in, I kept my distance, and dared not threaten any punishment when he returned. If passers-by had come along the road, I could have exerted my authority; but when all men are reduc'd to savagery, the stronger savage is king.

Nearing the orchard, I decided the only stratagem was to reveal truthfully to Trenoggin what had happened so that, with his greater authority, he could set off to rescue his ass and cart. But as we trailed up the track he spied us, and without waiting for a word of explanation, cried out that we were thieves who had sold his animal and dray; and taking his slave to be prime robber, began to belabour Alfonso with the blunt side of his cutlass. So violent were his drunken yells, that Daniel and Archibald stood up watching amid the fruit trees, and Priscilla came out shrieking to the door. Though frightened myself, I ran up to try to hold back the old Pirate, fearing there would be murder. And so there was, but not of the young slave: for of a sudden, Alfonso wrenched the cutlass from Trenoggin, and hack'd him bloody to the ground.

I was long enough upon the isle to know that for a slave to kill his Master is the final dreaded crime, unpardonable; and that, for the slave, the only alternative to instant death is the faint hope of escape and hiding. My good sense told me also that though I had done the slaves no special ill, because I was a witness to their deed, the next death would be my own. So I leap't up and ran, but glancing swiftly back, saw they did not pursue me; and were hacking at each other's fetters violently with the cutlass.

My duty, I knew, and my most prudent course, was to hasten to the nearest in authority and inform about them; indeed, did I not do so, I would be deemed an accomplice to their crime. And yet I fear'd to do this, not because of any love towards the slaves, but because I knew not where to turn. To the soldiers? What welcome would they give me? To Mr George? How could I trust his harsh brutality? Yet truth to say, this reasoning came after, and what carried my swift feet racing to the beach was only panick. I sought out the sea to hide, because it seemed furthest from this atrocious island.

The longer I lingered by the shore, the more I felt bereft and paralys'd. I am a man now, and would not, I hope, be such a coward, or so undecided; of which I shall have soon to make my dreadful proof. But then I was sixteen, and if not a boy — for my fate since I left the Highlands had promoted me in hard experience — I was yet one who, in terror, could not be all the man he wished.

Night came, and with it hunger; and such beasts are we, with animal needs which never leave us, that often our bellies rule our conduct, not our wills. And so I crept back toward the orchard, seeing no soul in the cold light of the moon.

Outside the hut, I found a horror: which was that the slaves had hack'd Trenoggin into morsels — this creature was not just slain, but quartered as by butchers. I shudder'd at this, but did not greatly fear any proximity of the slaves knowing full well that, after plundering the hut, they would make off to the scant security of the hills. And as to fear, I was by now in such terror as to be past fearing.

Yet when I crept into the hut, I froze: for nails clutch't me, and cries shrill'd. I tore at the flesh and voice, and fell in a tangle of wild limbs and sobbing, till I thought 'twas Priscilla, but still gripp'd.

'*Obeah, obeah,*' she cried.

'Nay, lie still, 'tis I!'

'Is spook, no!'

'Nay — Alexander!'

And we clutch'd there in a terror till the girl, wrung dry by sobs, lay panting and moaning in the dark. I tried to ask where the slaves had gone, but could get no coherence from her. And when I sought to rise and cook for sustenance, she clung to me with such groans and graspings that I forbore, and tried to soothe her.

Those who know not Calvinists say that our youth are denying prudes, or else hypocrite lechers. This is not so: we cherish womankind as anyone, yet believe, for the beauty of our lives here and hereafter, that we must come to a woman with a single pledge. Besides this faith, my hope had always been that I would bank down all fires of the flesh till they could burn with the heat not only of holiness, but love. But this was not to be; for that night, almost as if Fate commanded Instinct, I became lover to this dark slave.

I know my sin, for this mating was unhallow'd either by soul or heart; and for yielding my first fruits to a savage, I can ask no pardon. All I say is that no lust was present, but what seemed, on that fearful night, the clutching of two frightened children.

The Mole

WE WERE woken by soldiers, for a carter, coming at sunrise into Joie, had seen from the road dogs tearing at something by Trenoggin's hut, and so come up and made his horrible discovery. Fearing to explore further – which might have warned us of immediate danger – he had run into Joie, we hearing nothing, and so exhausted we thought it was still night.

The soldiers would hear no explanations, but bound us and dragg'd us into Joie, where we were flung separately into dungeons. And as I feared, it was Mr Johnstone who came to me saying I would stand trial on two capital charges, and one lesser: on complicity in murder and escape of slaves, and for lying with a slave woman not my own. This he told me with chill relish; and I discern'd in his venom that hatred, beyond all other, that a Lowland Scot can cherish for his Highland brother.

I asked who would try me, and he said a Justice; and at this I was even more afraid. I have explained how, in St Laughter, so small it is there is no Governor, and hence not any Courts. Only grave cases fetch over judges from Resurrection, his headquarter, the lesser (such as my own) being tried by Planters who are also Magistrates; and if the Governor's justice is a harsh one, it is methodical; but the Magistrate's is but a Whim.

The soldiers who brought me food were honest enough, with a rough pity. They told me the hunt was up for Daniel,

Archibald and Alfonso, with foragers and hounds. These slave hunts are an amusement to the soldiers, and to the planters' sons who, having no foxes on the island, join in the frolic. But if the slaves are not soon discover'd, the hunt is fast abandon'd; for the highlands of St Laughter are rough and troublesome, making hard going, and bringing more pain than pleasure in the chase.

Before my trial, I was put to torture, which was to be beat about naked with red-hotted metal thongs. In my agony, I cried out why did they thus ravish me, for God knows they had concocted crimes enough. But I found Johnstone wished most to lay on me a felony committed before my arrival in St Laughter, and one that in his dark heart, was greater: namely that I had been a rebel, and had borne arms in Scotland against King George. After hours of agony, I confess'd to this high treason (promising to myself that, if ever I escaped them, I would commit the treachery they had made me swear to). This yielding of truth to pain, I relate with shame; but beg leave only to be judged for it by him who has been tortured, and kept silence.

I expected my trial would last a minute, since they held written confessions of everything I had not done. But here I understood not St Laughter, and how, in their universal tedium, and lack of all entertainment save for liquor, dice and fornication, a trial was pretty to them as a play. I was wash'd and dress'd neatly by the soldiers in the morning, and told, with many a jest, how Priscilla had been sold to an old planter, and how they wished their pay was such as to let them speak up at the auction for her. They gave me a hearty break-fast, and even rum; and for the first time I was to notice what I frequently have since, which is that kind of corrupt affection

68

that men have for those, especially the innocent, whom they purpose to destroy.

There is no courtroom in Joie, and my trial was held in the mess of the officers, at the barracks. The Magistrate, Mr Newbury (he who had bought Priscilla), was a jovial old fellow, much fondled by the military, whom he entertained cordially on his plantation. The officers, all in the pink of their regalia, chatted and laugh'd with young bloods and maidens, sons and daughters of the planters. The soldiers kept guard on nothing, and slaves in their best attire handed round wine and sweetmeats. Indeed, it was a merry scene for all save I – and for long I seemed so forgotten, that one could scarcely believe death hung over the assembly.

But death did not visit it for when, towards midday, they turned towards the trial (as to a sad interruption in their celebration), it seemed Lt Johnstone, who was chosen prosecutor (I had no defender), was anxious that I should live, but live for a fate he believed more ignoble. For speaking up, as if on my behalf, he begged Mr Newbury to consider that tho' I was a deserter guilty of two capital crimes, and two of lust and robbery, my worser one was to be a rebel, and by this I should be chiefly judged. For rebellion, the penalty was also death. But Mr Newbury might please consider that when I committed this evil, grave and absolute though it was, I was a lad, doubtless led astray by corrupters. And therefore my fit punishment should be the same as that inflicted on Scots rebels not deemed worthy of the gallows, which was to be a slave. To confer Justice in the King's name, the Lieutenant concluded, was Mr Newbury's sacred duty; but the circumstances of the case were such that in this instance it might be tempered with the Mercy of sparing my life, and taking away my freedom.

Mr Newbury seemed much affected by this discourse, blew his nose, refreshed himself with wine, and turning to me (as if for the first time beholding me) asked had I anything to say.

'Sir,' said I, 'of the crimes imputed to me I am guilty of only two, neither of which merits death or slavery. That I deserted ship, 'tis true; but pray, sir, consider . . .'

'Ah! You admit it!' cried the Justice. 'Note that well,' he said, gazing round the assembly. 'He avows the less to excuse the greater, but we shall not be deceived!' and they all murmur'd approbation.

'Aye, sir, I admit it,' I declared. 'And as to lying with the wench, I own that too.'

'Fie!' exclaimed Newbury, his eye bulging, his neck bursting from his lace kerchief. 'Fie on your lewdness before the ladies!' (who all hid simpering behind fans, while their swains glared at me in manly revulsion). 'Fie on your shamelessness,' he shouted, 'parading your lechery and sweaty fornications on a savage!'

I withstood their glares, and asked if I might continue; and perhaps hoping for more of lechery, he did not deny me.

'As for the capital crimes I am accused of,' I went on, 'I laid no hand on Trenoggin, nor did I help the slaves to flee.'

'Ha!' cried the Justice. 'And who says so?'

'I, sir, who was there.'

'Aye – you: you who were there to witness both crimes by your own admission!' and he gazed on the indignant faces of the sweaty room.

'There remains the charge of rebellion against our King,' I continued firmly. 'Of the truth of this you can best judge by referring to my uncle, Mr Zachary Troon of Mortar, in Ayrshire, who must tell you it is false.'

At this Mr Newbury shewed some surprise and doubt, crying, 'Ho! Mr Troon of Mortar, the molasses chandler! A worthy fellow, known to us all here in St Laughter. And he would be uncle to a reprobate?'

'He is my uncle, sir.'

'You claim him uncle! Does he claim you nephew?'

But at this there was some muttering with the officers at his table, then hard nodding, and the Magistrate addressed me with an ornate gravity.

'The accusations all stand proven,' he declared, 'and from this instant, your freedoms are forfeit, you are a slave.' Here he paused, gazing already at me as I were some other. 'My sentence is absolute, save for two contingencies. It must be confirmed by His Excellency, to whom an account of our proceedings will be transmitted at Resurrection. And in justice to the good repute of Mr Zachary Troon, if not to your own for you have none, I shall have enquiry made concerning you in Ayrshire.'

'But sir,' I cried out loud. 'To be a slave . . .'

'Silence!' he thundered. 'Let this be borne away!'

Mr Johnstone asked him whither. To the auction block, or was I designate to any special plantation? A wise look overcame the Magistrate's judicious features. 'Since his condemnation is in some measure conditional,' he said, 'and I am its legal author, 'twould be well this slave be consigned to my estates till all is made definite and final.' With these words he arose, and a lively hubbub, and I was borne away as if I did not exist at all.

And so I became a slave, a condition so rare among my countrymen that they might care, even if they wish not to believe, to know of it. True it is there are white slaves enough in the West Indies, chiefly Irishmen and Scots; but being men mostly of a lesser sort, and silenced by illiteracy and obscurity, there is little interest about them, or the possibility of satisfying it. Besides, there is this paradox: that England has sent Celts as slaves to the Caribbean now for greater than a century, especially in Cromwellian times. But their descendants here, now freed, and shamed of their ancestry, will not admit to how their fathers came here, and have turned patriot.

The white slaves of the Corsairs in Africa are better known of, being often men — and women too — of substance; but because our fleets operate in Moorish waters, and their freedom is sometimes won by ransoming or bombardment, they are thought by most to be the only Britons who are so humiliated. The more so because, when an alien nation like the Arabs enslaves a Briton, their fate seems an indignity never to be borne; but this is not felt when Britons enslave their kind, who are enfolded in a silence.

He who may fear that to make whites slaves among the blacks could create a kind of Republick of the oppress'd, can reassure himself; for the truth is, that to share the indignity forced upon the blacks, only makes the white slaves hate them more. For the white thinks the black born slave-fodder, and he not; so that to be reduced to the blacks' condition spurs his loathing. Nor need there be much fear that even among the white slaves, any unity can be born of misery to nurture a rebellion. For the slave desperately hates the slave; and through treachery to his fellow, seeks the favour of the Master.

What remains peculiar to this condition, and most horrible, is to become a being that is none. In vain does the slave, in the first days of his new condition, say to his heart, 'Yet I remain a man!' But he does not. For what is a man? A man does not consist only of body, brain and spirit; but in the exercise of all these faculties according to, and in some measure however small, his own desires and will. But the wishes and will of slaves are, save in sleep, his master's. When I was a sailor, almost press-gang'd to a ship, I thought myself 'a slave' and said as much. Little did I then know how vast, within the tyranny of Captain Peters, was my freedom!

As to the free whose business it is to deal with slaves, they too must lose their freedom: which is any choice whatever of compassion or, indeed, of human feeling even most minimal, towards another. I swear it is harder to love a slave than love a horse. For to beat a horse is not to beat one of his own kind, and hence himself; and to beat a man without any reflection – without, indeed, the possibility of any – is to be forced to hate him. Now, a choice of hatreds still leaves some part of freedom; but to hate by necessity, is to be deprived of all of it.

Thus, those who misused us could scarcely be called cruel, or rarely so. To slay a hen to eat it is not cruel, or so regarded; to lash a slave to duty, neither. Indeed, to show any small tenderness to a slave is crueller still; for it may deceive him as to his true condition, and make later cruelties seem more terrible.

I was put to work on a new mole that Mr Newbury, tho' a planter, (his estate has named Meadowsweet), had contracted with the admiralty to build onto Joie harbour. We climbed the hills, hew'd rocks, carried them down in baskets, and dropp'd them into the sea. All our gang were whites, for the races must not work together; and the overseers said we were even idler than the Africans.

73

There was none in the gang that I could love, and few I did not think inside my heart (heaven help me!) to be worthy of their fate! Perhaps, in happier conditions, I might have made mates among them. But slavery teaches you that human brotherhood has much to do with soap, a full belly, and the possibility of free utterance and motion.

My only consolation came, unexpectedly, from the soldiers. Perhaps they felt I had been wronged, and they responsible for it; perhaps, since their own condition was hard enough, they took some pity on one harder. But they would bring me small gifts down to the mole when they went swimming there; and because they were rough and hearty with the overseers (who also feared their temper and weapons, as all lesser persons in Joie did), this slight intercourse was not forbidden me.

I could also snatch some converse with the sailors on the small boats in the harbour who, because I was young and sturdy, would sometimes hire me from the overseers (which was forbidden, tho' well bribed) for petty duties. It was thus I met Marrowbone (he owned no other name), who was to play a large part in my story.

I believe that Marrowbone had Africk blood, for he was swart, and his limbs moved in their cat-like fashion. But this I would never dare say aloud, for he cried out continually his detestation of the blacks. He was not a native of St Laughter, but of Resurrection; and because, even on those small adjacent islands of the Caribbean, each seems to have grown its own peculiar accent, he was much mock'd for his speech in Joie, but did not mind it; saying that people of so insignificant a smudge as was St Laughter, could not tell fair speech from foul, knowing no better.

Because the tasks he gave me were not hard, and he allowed me some small leisure in them, I began to believe he had some purpose in his benevolence, since a slave learns that none does him a kindness, save perhaps by sloth. And indeed, he had all the time a way of eyeing me, in a speculative bent, as if there was something he meditated to unfold.

Sure enough, one afternoon when he had careen'd his skiff, some distance outside the harbour, to scrape it there, he lower'd his knife, offered me a cigar (the prize if caught smoking one was fifty lashes), and said, did I like the condition of a slave. At this I could only smile, sadly enough; and he, smiling too, continued:

'A slave has three choices, boy. One is slavery itself, which will kill him, unless he is a household pet, before he is thirty. The next is escape, which means torture and death if captured, or slow starvation in a short and conditional freedom.'

I owned this was true enough, and waited. But then he, first gazing round at the sky, as if looking for a bird, asked had I ever heard of Captain Nayle? To this I rejoined guardedly that the murder'd Trenoggin had told me of him. 'Aye,' said Marrowbone, 'and how did he speak of him?' 'Well, he spoke of him as being a pirate.' 'Aye, lad: but what sort of a pirate did he say?' To this I replied that since the Cornishman had been himself one (or had so averr'd), he had not spoken ill of Mr Nayle.

'Nor should he,' cried Marrowbone, with some vehemence. 'For Nayle is an honest fellow, and a seaman *sans pareil.*'

I asked him how he knew so.

At this he looked dark, as if it was I who had broached the topick. But then he smil'd pleasantly, showing his teeth, and continued, 'For that, lad, you make take my word; and indeed, those of many good seamen in the pool here at St Laughter.'

I said I would not doubt his word.

'Nay, lad, I trust not!' he exclaimed. Then lowering his voice, tho' none was about to hear him, he said, 'Nayle has been the salvation of many a good man in trouble.'

I could see, of course, where he was heading to, but was bent on prudence. For should he make me (as I divined) some offer of service with Nayle, how could I know he was really a familiar of the Captain? And how could I tell he might not denounce my interest to the overseers? And even more favouring silence was that if I had still some hope of the enquiries about my case setting me free, was it not safer to remain a slave, unjustly condemn'd, than to condemn myself beyond all hope of justice by embracing piracy? Perhaps Marrowbone read my mind, for all he said further was, 'These are matters to be ponder'd on by anyone in a desperate situation.' Though when we had scraped the boat, and were sailing back into the harbour, he looked up a moment at the crags overhanging Joie and said, as if to himself, 'Aye, some of the sturdiest buccaneers in the Caribbean seas are recruited among escap'd slaves off the islands.'

Among the most dismal vexation of the slave's lot (if any is more so than another) is that peering at us, and probing, of the free. Most freemen, it is true, so accept slaves as not to notice them; but others (especially the young, and of these, particularly females), have a kind of joy at staring on us for hours, even following us along; and I have known those who reach out, in a sort of infernal ecstasy, for the pleasure of plucking at a slave's sleeve. To this he may become hardened, but not altogether; since humiliation is an even greater pain to bear than cruelty.

Among those who came to spy on us as we were labouring on the mole were chiefly the planters' children: that is, not the elder sons and daughters, who I doubt not had fitter occupations, nor the infants, who feared us, tho' God knows we could do them no harm; but mostly the kind half lamb, half ewe who, tho' they had their own house slaves to walk by them and almost lift up each foot for them to take a step, seemed dazzl'd by our sweaty toil.

Or sometimes, when they cruis'd about the bay in skiffs, sporting and fishing, they would swoop in beside the mole and circle it, shouting and skylarking beside our heavy silence. And once, when they called our overseer, he came back to tell us they wanted men to dive for shells. For true, the seashells of St Laughter are of a special brilliance, and famous, 'twas said, even to the scholarly of England. But because of the dangerous fishes in the harbour, these shell seekers would not want themselves to dive; nor even allow it to their domestic slaves who, being house trained, were valuable.

None of us was anxious for the privilege save I and another scatterbrain, for whom the joy of being a while unshackl'd and to swim, outweighed our slight fears at the venture. And I had also the joyful conceit of a novice: for this was one of the useful arts I had learned while working for Trenoggin, and now believed myself a very porpoise. So we both plunged in and fortune favoured us, for we brought up so many beauties that the girls cried out in raptures, and even the boys seemed pleased; though they continued to take all the credit, seizing the shells from us at the boat's edge, and handing them to their ladies as if, like Neptune, they had brought them up.

I was growing tired of this, for the sea press'd on my lungs; when of a sudden, my companion screamed when a shark took him, nipping off a leg. But while he struggled, none made to help him, and he soon went in a great red pool. As for me, having no wish to follow him, and being far off from the mole, I sought not to swim there, but heav'd myself unbidden into the nearest boat.

For a while they did not notice me, being so intent on the murder in the sea; but when they did, were horrified, and their slaves made to thrust me over with an oar. Till I, clinging desperate to the edge, was urged by my guardian angel to cry out, 'But you would not lose one of Newbury's slaves!'

At this a damsel of perhaps fifteen (but I know not) cried out to her swain, 'Stop them, Horatio!' and the youth she spoke to, who was an older fellow and the man among them, chid the slaves to let me lie athwart the stern, till we reach'd shore. 'See, I have saved him for you, Diana,' the boy said; and the girl, thanking him, 'My father would not have forgiven me his loss.'

Then the youth came closer, standing akimbo eyeing me, with a glance of some displeasure on his handsome face. 'Marry, he stinks,' he said. 'I trust he does not incommode you too exceedingly, Di.'

'Nay, so long as he stays where he is put,' said she, obligingly.

'So you are slave to this lady's father, boy,' he said to me.

'Aye, sir, to Newbury,' said I.

He lash'd me across the face with a cane he carried. '*Mr* Newbury,' he said.

'To Mr Newbury, sir.'

He nodded, and the girl said, 'Do not strike him, Horatio.

He is so young – and look: he has found us these pretty shells.'

'Aye,' said the boy '—pretty shells,' and frown'd and turned his back on me.

But the girl seemed curious to continue parley, which I feared; for no word I could say would find favour with them. And so, to her questions I mumbled only short humble answers, seeking to play the loon. Though when I was put ashore upon the mole, and shackl'd up again, the girl threw me a little smile, sweet, false and painful to my feeling.

The Heiress

WHEN the overseer called me, some days later, and said I was
to go to Meadowsweet, to Mr Newbury's, to be servant
there, I knew instantly it was because of the girl. Six months
before, when I was innocent of all tribulations, I might have
thought this was because of some fondness that she had for
me; but now I knew better, or thought I did; and determined
she wanted me for a pet, or for some devilment, since I could
not believe of any honest commerce 'twixt a freeman and a
slave.

Meadowsweet is on the further, or eastern shore of St
Laughter, and to reach it you must travel round the island
because of the sheer peaks that form its backbone. I was carried in a cart, still shackl'd, with stores that an overseer, with
slaves to help him, had come into Joie to fetch for Mr
Newbury. This man did not treat me ill, but said nothing to
me, nor did the slaves, all of which were black.

This journey, which took all day till nightfall, gave me a
better knowledge of the island: which is indeed a paradise,
whatever its inhabitants may have made of it. The lawns
slope down to the sea as in our Lowlands, only richer, but the
crags are more ragged and volcanic than in our glens, and
thickly furr'd with a sodden foliage. There are no villages except for Joie; tho' each plantation is, so to say, a village, with the
big house, the barns and storehouses for sugar, and barracks
for the slaves. The people everywhere move steady and

methodickal, like ants: I mean that, tho' there is not the sharp energy of the North (because of the heat), there is a continual groan of labour and none dare seem idle.

My joy can be judged that the first face I saw when we reached Meadowsweet, was Priscilla's; but this did not last long, for she turn'd away from me, as if I was unknown. I was taken to a slave-hut which was less barbarous than what I was used to on the Mole, being bare, but decent. And two surprises were that I was unshackl'd, and that the white slaves were mixed here with the black, though they were more than we. I was told by the overseer to wait, and make ready to be seen by Mr Newbury. I did not speak to the other slaves when they came in, nor they to me; I out of cautiousness, and they, no doubt, to show that contempt which is ever the newcomer's due.

At length I was called before my Master, to his study, which was a long room, with a verandah, facing on the starlight of the bay, and with that untidiness of ease which betokens a rich man's dwelling in a house without a wife. I stood before him in my rags, but clean, and he in a tropick shirt, breeches and barefoot, and with one hand holding a brandy glass, and the other picking at a toe.

'Well, boy,' said he, eyeing me, 'the first thing to be done with you is put you in fair clothes.'

'Aye, sir,' said I.

'Now, as to your duties,' he continued. 'We will start you in the kitchen, and if you are no better than for that, you will remain there. But if you show diligence and duty, we may promote you to serving boy about the house.'

'Aye sir,' I said once more.

'There is one thing I should tell you, if you do not wish to

lose your testicles,' Mr Newbury said pleasantly. 'The overseer will show you to old Martha, and with her you may in-
dulge your lusts as freely as you wish. But if you are caught
with any of the girl-slaves, why! you will be castrated!' and he
smiled. 'And if,' he went on, 'you should so much as touch, as
look at, a free woman . . . why! You will lose first your privy
organs, then your life.'

I made no reply.

'You do not answer, boy.'

'Aye, sir,' I said. But while he was speaking to me, gazing
up under his lids and quaffing brandy, I was wondering: for
why should a Master send for a slave to tell him this, he who is
too great a man, and gives all orders by his overseer?

'Boy!' he said suddenly. 'Because I condemn'd you, you do
not wish me ill?'

I halted, then said to him, 'Sir, I wish only that when you
confirm the truth of what I told you, you shall set me free.'

'Aye – bravely said. And *are* you nephew to Mr Zachary?'

'Sir, I have sworn it to you. What else have I, till proof
comes, but my word?'

'None, 'tis true. Yet tell me what you know of Mortar,
and the molasses trade.'

This was not much, but I told him my little store, and he
asked me some questions, in a teasing way, to which I knew
not the answers, he shaking his head and smiling. 'Aye,' he
said then, when I grew silent, 'but all that could be gossip, or
thieves' tales.'

I flush'd, but stood my ground, though fearful.

'Well, to your quarters,' he said rising. But he stopp'd me at
the door and, much to my astonishment, offered me a glass of
spirit. When I declined warily, he grew vex'd, and forced it on

me. Now shutting the door carefully, he paced about the room, till he darted a finger at me, and he said, 'My daughter tells me that you are brave.'

'I hope I am, sir.'

'Well! You are a slave here, and you have your duty. But if you wish to earn your freedom, I demand more from you than duty.'

'Sir?'

'Yes!' He looked at me closely, peering as if to find some secret in me, and said, 'If ever you are near my daughter, watch her!'

'But, sir, I . . .'

'Yes, she must be watched.' He stood still, thinking of I knew not what. 'I cannot say all to you now, boy. Not all, but this I will tell you.' Then, looking fierce and bitter, he cried in a low voice, 'But this is a *wicked* island, and there are *evil* creatures on it!' I kept silent, much amazed, and he also for a while. Then he said, 'She must be protected!' He took the glass from me, almost as tho' I had sought to steal it, and dismissed me abruptly, turning his bent back.

Out in the courtyard I saw no one, and so unused was I to making any movement without orders, that I waited in the night for a sharp cry of command. But instead there came hissings from out the darkness, and I heard Priscilla.

'Quiet, boy,' she whispered. 'Hey! You know why I not speak to you before?'

'Is it forbidden?'

'Is *prohibit*, man, specially to you. Me not allow to say nuttin to you never, you understand?'

'Kiss me, Priscilla.'

'Boy, you crazy? Stop it, now!' But she was in my arms,

light and firm. 'Hey, you know what?' she said, pushing me away. 'We goin' to have a baby, me and you.'

'No!'

'What you mean, "no"? You goin' to say now he not yours?'

'Yes but . . . Priscilla, I can not believe this!'

'*I* can – feel here!'

'What will become of it, Priscilla?'

'Slave child!' she said softly. 'Out in the sugar cane, tho' maybe I get him in the house . . . Hey! I bet they crack their guts guessin' who he dad.'

'Perhaps they will think 'twas old Trenoggin.'

'Blood clot, you nice! Hé, all that old man could do was clutch and fumble. He no more juice in he than a dried cane. Kiss me, boy, quick, I go now.'

'I shall see you again?'

'*See* me, sure, but *speak* to me . . . well, let me choose the time.' Her voice fell almost silent under the stars. 'Next time I talk to you, I tell you the message from the boys.'

'Daniel and . . .?'

'*Quiet!* Up in the hills, they're livin'.' Then she was gone.

I found my way to the slave hut, where the men were settling down for sleep. Some were throwing dice, which were cut ingeniously from the hard rind of the coconut; and I was surprised to see them throwing coins until I guessed that, harsh though are the rules against the slaves having any possession, in domestic slavery there is always matter for corruption. Some lads were singing, and had made a rude fiddle out of casks and the gut of beasts. On the cot beside me was a huge fellow of large lip and eye, who beat solemnly upon a hollow drum, made from a chopp'd trunk and the hairy skin of goat; he playing it with an intensest concentration until, breaking off and looking up at me, he said, 'Bo-bo, I think I see you face before.'

'Not mine, friend, I am sure,' said I.

'Yes, bo-bo, was you face. When I come off that pretty ship you carry me here in.'

'You were on the slaver?'

'Yes, one of your passenger, was me.'

Foolish and useless tho' it was, I could not measure my embarrassment at this: honest, by regret of what I had done to him, but vain, because I was now cast down like he. So I said, 'But how came you learned to speak our tongue so fast?'

He smiled at me, head on one side. 'Ho, some of us speak English on the Coast . . . and others is learning it fast now.'

'You have an English name?'

'No, thank God: but you may call me Bandele. What your name?'

'Alexander.'

'Alexander. Nh – hn!'

'Are there any more Africans here in the house?'

'No, poor fellows, they dying in the cane. They pick me out because I can interpret. Also, the old Bastard like my drumming.'

'Mr Newbury?'

'Yes. The old Fuck-arse.'

'Be prudent, Bandele!'

'The old Shit-eat.'

The door flung open, and it was the overseer. 'Half an hour for Martha, then lock-up' he cried out.

Several of the men rose, and I came with them tho' more by curiosity than lust. The overseer took us to a small hut by itself where we waited outside, while each man entered singly. When only Bandele and I were left, he said, 'So long I shut my eye, she heaven,' and stepped in. He stayed longer than most, and when he emerg'd, said, 'Elephant is sweeter,' and made off.

Martha was a mulatto, perhaps forty, and indeed no beauty. I pleaded my youth not to offend her, asked could I but converse with her a while, and she seemed not offended, perhaps because fatigu'd. 'Chow, boy, why not?' she cried merrily, and offered me a rum. I asked her to tell me of the life here at Meadowsweet.

'Well, is like so,' the elderly harlot answered. 'Mr Newbury, one time, was king-pin of this island. But his wife – she a Spain lady – run away to Mr Wilson, he of Valentine, into Eng-land; what is more bad, he wife take away not jus' her pussy, but a whole heap of money too. Poor Mr Newbury, he tabanca, see, he totalbe; and all is left to he, is Miss Diana, who like the apple of he eye.

'But this apple, it have like worm: for let me tell you, Miss Diana, she a bitch: I mean like vix-en. She tyrant of the plantation, and what she need is husband who t'ump her some, like give she a pair o' licks.'

'Has not Miss Diana suitors?'

'Ho! Well, what you expec'? Mr Newbury, he still loaded, and there's plenty studs to sigh. But trouble is, Miss Diana she sweet for young Horatio Wilson, who jus' come back ear out of Cu-bah. But to Mr Newbury, any Wilson, he like snake.'

'So he will seek to prevent their union?'

'Well, boy, by law he can – he the father, he hold the power. But what law ever stop hot pussy? Please tell me that!'

A yell from the overseer interrupted this intelligence. 'Get off her!' he cried, so apologising to Miss Martha, I hastened to the hut, where the overseer flung me in and locked the door.

In the morning, washing at the goat troughs, I could see the wide extent of Meadowsweet; and truly the spectacle was one to strike wonder by its beauty. The big house was on a cliff falling to the sea, whose waves, from this height, crawl'd lazily and were inaudible. The out-buildings fell away in stages, as in our hill villages, and the sugar fields were laid into terraces hemmed with rocks. The slaves were already out, bent in labour, their cutlasses flashing occasionally as they hew'd, with shouts and cracks of the overseers muted from this distance. On all this a cool sun shone, it was so early. And I could not but think of what a jewel St Laughter must have been before Europe gave it its saint's name, and the Caribes roamed on its pastures in the perfection of their ignorance of the world.

After a breakfast of yams, I was taken to be fitted with a livery, and look'd a very popinjay when they had done with all the tucks and hemmings. For one of the perversities of the planters is that tho' they deny all but the meanest of brute satisfactions to their house-slaves, they dress them in a style thoroughly provoking. I am no prude (at least, so I hope), but I confess when I saw in a mirror how they had encas'd me, I almost blush'd; for had I walked thus attired down the streets of Mortar, I would have been mock'd, or stoned. But none seemed to find my appearance remarkable, and all gazed at me candidly, as farmers do at the fine points of a ram.

I was carrying sweet corn from the kitchen, and entering the pass-door into the masters' quarters, for the dining-room, when I saw Miss Diana on the stair. 'Come hither, slave,' she said proudly, but with a sort of horrid daintiness, and I approach'd, feeling a fool, and wishing with all my heart I could chastise her for her impertinence. But serene in her lofty posture, and, I will own, beauty, she survey'd me appraisingly then said, 'Pretty slave! But do not forget, ever forget, that I took the shackles off your feet and can screw them back in an instant. Open that door!' Then she bid me to the verandah, where I was to swing the great fan; and she reclined there on a ratten sofa, teasing me with a glimpse of ankle and of throat.

By and by there arrived Mr Horatio, caracoling on a horse; and tho' his slave ran beside him, he called to me to hold his stirrup. When he trod on my hand, and dug hard, I made no sound; but opened the door to the verandah with a bow. He kiss'd Miss Diana's hand prettily; and when I made to withdraw, she frown'd me to continue fanning. This was in part, I knew, the trick girls have to plague a suitor with the presence of another man, even a boy and slave; and also that curiosity I had already noticed, which is that in the presence of their slaves, the owners speak as if before children, esteeming neither to have ears.

'La, Horatio,' she said. 'I declare nothing happens in St Laughter. How I sigh for England and far more, for France and Spain.'

'But Di! I have told you you should order your Father to send you over, or at least let you see substantial islands, such as Cuba. For a girl, dearest, who knows only these abandoned places, is no more than a sweet barbarian.'

'Fie, Horatio! How can my Father let me go to England where your lecher of a Papa has carried off my poor Mamma!'

'By permitting you, my heart, to go there in the company

of one who most cherishes you!' and he took up her hand again, kissing it.

But now, at this contact of the flesh, they both glanc'd at me; and the youth cried, 'Be off with you, fellow!' so I departed. I helped the young planter's slave to carry his horse away and loose the saddle, and for water. 'He a right blood-clot bastard,' his faithful slave confided.

'He often visits here?'

'Since he come back, he try to. But if old Newbury catch he, is talk of du-el. That why we hang hid up the track, waitin' till we see the old feller ridin' out jus' now.'

When I was sent to gather beans, Priscilla contriv'd to talk to me by hanging washing on the nearby hedges, speaking soft as if she did not see me. 'Those boy want to get away,' she said, glancing upward at the hills. 'Off this island! You see a way?'

'But how have you heard from them, Priscilla?'

'By a Caribe.'

'A who?'

'A Red Indian. Hey! You ignorant? Was Caribe here before Colombo come.'

'But they are all gone, Priscilla! Dead long ago!'

'Oh? Well, maybe they not. Maybe is some up in the hills, and maybe Daniel meet with them, and have a chat.'

'This must be an invention, girl. Why do you tell me lies?'

'Oh – so I lying? Well, perhaps you see!'

'Daniel is working his *obeah* on you from the hills!' I said to her in my disbelief.

'That maybe true, as well,' said she.

I was put to scouring pans with Bandele, and thought I would ask him about this sorcery. For if it was true the superstition came from Africa, he might know more of it. But when I broach'd on the topic, he eyed me in displeasure. 'Who has been saying to you what I do?' he asked me fiercely.

'No one, Bandele.'

'Well, I think you may shut your mouf,' said he.

But that mystery was more nearly resolv'd when, late in the evening, I was called once more to the presence of Mr Newbury, and was amaz'd to find Bandele standing there. My Master, 'twas clear, had been at the bottle, but his gravity had mellowed in proportion.

'Boy,' he said, pointing the neck of his bottle at me, 'you are a Scot?'

'Aye, sir.'

'And being a Scot, you would be a Presbyterian?'

'Aye, sir,' said I.

'And Knox: he is the originator of all faith?'

'Nay, sir: Calvin is our Teacher.'

'Aye, aye; and Calvin, *he* is the originator?'

'Why, no, sir: 'twas, as you surely know, our blessed Saviour.'

Here he took a swig. 'So, boy; and before Him?'

'The Jews, sir. The revelation of God to Moses.'

'And before?'

'We are taught, sir, that human history began in Eden.'

'Aye. But see, boy, where that carries us. For it leaves us with two problems unresolved by Holy Writ. What were the world's thoughts before Moses? And what of the lands where no Jew ever set his feet?

'Sir?'

'Had they no revelation?'

'In truth, I know not, sir.'

Mr Newbury looked mightily pleas'd, and turned to the son of Africa. 'Teach him,' said he.

Bandele let off a mighty grin, and I was amaz'd at his familiarity with our Master. 'We all have our Magick,' he replied. 'You yours, we ours.'

Mr Newbury nodded. 'Lad,' he said, turning to me again, 'we must not despise the apprehensions of the savages; the more so as, in St Laughter, we are surrounded by them.'

At this blasphemy I could find no words; only supposing that the familiarity of the planters with the slaves could induce not only contempt, but a part of hidden admiration.

'And you, boy,' said Newbury to Bandele, 'will you work well the charm that you have promised me?'

'Be sure of that, Mastah,' said the African, and they looked at each other privily, as if sharing some wisdom beyond my poor understanding. Then, turning to me, the smile of congratulation to Bandele vanishing, he cried out angrily, 'Why did you not tell me he was here?'

'Who, sir?'

He raised his fist. 'Do not trifle, or you shall be whipp'd! I told you to watch my daughter: why have you not done so as I ordered?'

'But sir! Am I to spy upon Miss Newbury?'

He dealt me a sudden blow. 'Not spy on anyone!' he cried, 'but tell all to me! I must know all, you understand me? All!'

Bandele, stepping forward humbly, held up a warning finger, and at this moment, with a flurry of skirts and petulation, there shot in on us Miss Diana, who glared at us slaves, crying out in a flashing dudgeon, 'Father, despatch them! I must speak with you!' At a wave from our Master we bowed and slunk out, but when the door closed Bandele gripp'd my arm to hold me still, and I could spy his grin flashing by a chink of light.

'You must not chatter with the slaves!' we heard Miss Diana cry. 'You corrupt them to idleness with their deceitful follies!'

'Even so? 'Twere better, daughter, to chatter with slaves than with a profligate poltroon.'

We heard the crack of a stamping foot. 'How dare you speak so of one like Horatio!'

'Of whom you soon recognised my description.'

'He is my beloved!'

'"Beloved"! He loves Meadowsweet and its acres well enough.'

'Fie, Father, for crying greed on a tender and honourable man! And has he not of all of Valentine for his birthright?'

'Has he? Who knows which son, or which bastard, the thieving lecher Wilson has willed it to?'

Bandele clutch'd me, and we tiptoed out to the yard. Here he let out a low laugh, and whispered, 'I think Miss Diana be surprise when she see Mr Horatio eye-socket without eye-ball.'

'You plan him some evil, Bandele?'

The African laughed again. 'Mr Man, I am a good slave, and I obey my Mastah. Come! Let us go into our palace.'

Sleep would not come to me in the slave hut that night, for I felt evil hung on the plantation. I puzzled my brain again as to how I could escape from all this horrid island; and was thinking of Marrowbone (tho' I mistrusted him), when I became aware the branch rustling on the outer wall was not moved there by nature, for it was beating out a steady, watchful sound. I rose, and crept amid the snoring and pack'd bodies, towards the one barred window of the hut, and peered there into the night. What I took for two bright stars were eyes. I started violently, but a voice said, 'Quiet. Quiet, Alexander. I come from Daniel. Rise at first light when the hut is opened. Come straight to the goat-pen, and wait there for me.'

'Who are you?'

There was silence, and in the dark all I could see were the eyes, not blinking. 'I am Joalla, the Caribe,' the voice said to me.

The Caribe

I SLEPT not at all, and was afoot waiting for the overseer when the locks clattered. I should have remembered the folly of seeming eager for duty, for the overseer seized on me and made me tip out the cisterns of the house. But as soon as I thought safe, and having now only a brief moment before I would be yelled for in the kitchen, I made off (carrying a pail as if much occupied) towards the scented clamour of the goat-pen.

There was nobody, and I imagined that 'twas all . . . no, I knew it was not a dream, could never be; and looking up, as if my eyes were pulled by a compulsion, I saw framed against the cliff above the pen, hardly visible against the rock, a slender figure quite unknown to me. With my head bent as if in honest toil, I labour'd up towards this spot where a hand reached out, and drew me into a recess, or little cave.

The Caribe was slink and stringy, his skin bronzen, and naked save for a plaited belt that held a knife. His hair, banded at the forehead with a pink strip, fell black-blue to his shoulder. He stood motionless as if even a mosquito would not make him flicker, while he listened. His slanted eyes stared steady, the teeth of his open mouth were large, irregular and sharp, and his face, with high bones, wore ńo expression, unless it was of a fierce and watchful disdain. Truth to tell, he terrified me: I mean, more so than any African, for his peril seemed more inward and contained.

But his voice was soft, though it twanged strangely like a metal. He put a thin hand upon my shoulder, staring at me without a blink, and said. 'This is the message to you from Daniel. The soldiers are hunting him too close; he must away, and you must help him.'

'How can I, in my condition here?'

'You must help him,' the Caribe repeated, with a thin smile. 'Daniel has a plot as well. It is to take the girl to the hills, and so buy his freedom, and his friends'.'

'Which girl?'

He glanced down at the big house.

'But that can not be possible!' I cried.

'Quiet. To take off the girl. You must think of this, and I shall come again. Make haste. Daniel sends greetings, and the others.'

I was fearful and mistrustful, and I said to him, 'But how do I know you are come from him?'

'And how do you know that I do not?'

'Why should you not be a slave spying for Mr Newbury? Or for Wilson?'

This won me a look that made me tremble. 'No Caribe has ever been a slave!'

He stood glaring at me, then turned and strode off. But I ran after him and cried, 'I cannot believe this. There are no Caribes left on the whole island.'

'And I? What do I seem to you?'

'I know not. But no one who is not white speaks our language as you do.'

At this he nodded to me, as if I was one of little knowledge. 'Man,' he said, 'we have known you for two hundred years.'

I could think of nothing to this. And fell back upon, 'And you, too, wish to flee with us from the island?'

'No, I shall remain. This is our land, and we shall wait.' He flashed out his knife and prick'd it to my breast. Staring at me, he said, 'You do not fear, Alexander?'

'Yes, I fear.'

'Do not fear: Joalla tells you.' He took back the knife. 'Turn your back to me. Do not watch the path I take.'

I ran down the hill in a dazed flurry, and was beaten about the head in the kitchen for my absence. The only excuse I could think of for my tarrying was that I had been seiz'd by the colic, at which they all express'd loud disgust. So acting the idiot to mask my trepidation, I did my tasks silently until the cook told me the young Mistress bade me to the stable. This seemed to me strange, for I was not stable hand, nor did Miss Diana ever go there; for horses were brought to her all equipp'd, and stood by the steps outside the great door, that was made of mahogany.

I found she was dressed for riding, standing alone beside her mare. 'Alexander,' she said to me, with a charm that flicker'd like the tumble of a star, 'you have not forgotten all you owe me?'

'Nay, Miss Diana – never!'

'So that I can demand your trust, boy?'

'It is ever yours, lady,' said I, watching her close.

She gazed at me reflecting, then she said, 'I want today to go Valentine, to Mr Wilson. You shall come with me: but see, my Father – and indeed no one – is not to know where I have been. If you are asked whither we went, why! it was for exercise upon the beaches; and our delay will be because . . . because you had the folly to let the horse escape, while I was resting, and were idle in catching it again.'

'That will earn me a beating, Miss Diana.'

'Oh! And for me you would not suffer that?'

What was so strange in her, was that she said this large-eyed and without irony. 'Your orders are sacred to me,' I replied.

She darted me a glance, then holding out her foot for the stirrup, she hoisted up; and crying, 'Run, boy!' trotted briskly off. She took the slave track out onto the road, then cantered off to circle round the island. Down the hills and on the flat, I lost her, but caught her again panting on the rises up. 'Lazy lad!' said she as I overtook her, and gave me a smart flick of rebuke across the back.

Truth to say, a horrid thought was coming on me, encouraged by the sweaty heat: which was, what had I so much to lose if, in this lonely part of the country, I seiz'd on her, dragg'd her off, and did her violence? And then myself run off to the hills, or away to Nayle, the mysterious forgiving pirate! So much was I learning, by my slave life, that virtue lies, in so large part, in the opportunity, at least, of being virtuous; and of this a slave has none, so that his only freedom is to snatch boldly at vice.

And indeed, I could feel that she provok'd me: almost inviting me to wickedness. For when we halted at the first far glimpse of Joie, she sent me to a stream to fetch water for the jar hanging from her saddle; and when I brought it, she was lying prettily upon the bank, whence she looked up at me with such an enticement and, it seemed too, with some evil kind of hope that I might tumble, and then be tortured for it. Yea; but before I was put to torture, might she not be ravish'd, and flung into the sea? And I believe she understood this too; and that such was her malice, even to herself, at that instant she scarcely cared.

'Is Martha sweet?' she said, mocking me.

'I know not.'

'Oh, Alexander! Are you then such a boy?'

Since it must have been apparent to her, from the condition of my garments, that I was not, I did not reply, but looked at her as calmly as I could, though hovering now upon a violence. This she saw: and in a trice turning from lust into an innocence (and strange! this innocence seemed real), she murmur'd, 'Aye child, 'tis sad to be a slave,' and leapt up on her horse and cantered off.

We came weary to Valentine, at least I know I did; and was glad of refreshment with the slaves there while my mistress was closeted with her Horatio. But I had scarce time to eat, and none to rest, for they came soon out to the horses, to ride in to Joie.

I shudder'd a little to see the town again, the gateway to all my misfortunes. Yet I was pleased to see ships, and free men moving free, though I was not one. My mistress and her lover went down on the quay, and stepped up on a craft there, leaving me to hold their nags. From the sailors I learned 'twas Mr Wilson's, and that it served his family for their journeyings about the islands.

This gave me a thought . . . was Miss Diana planning some elopement? Her caution in coming here, and lies prepared for her father, the two men's hatred, and this visit on the boat with Wilson, all made me wonder. But I hoped, if 'twere so, 'twere not today; for surely I would be whipp'd to death by Newbury if they made off; and what of the half promise I had made to the Caribe, to carry back to Daniel, concerning her?

And now, as if he knew that I expected him, Marrowbone appeared, and spoke to me easily as if the hints that he had made (concerning Captain Nayle) had been but yesterday, and that he knew I was by now all loaded with my reply. And on an impulse, I took him apart (giving the reins to a mariner to hold), and said that I, and slaves I had commerce with by secret emissaries, in their fortress up in the hills, were all of a mind to join Nayle if Marrowbone would tell us how; all this, with the reservation in my mind that if Marrowbone betray'd me to my owners, I would say that, in my duty to them, I had sought to trick him into an avowal of his nearness to the pirates.

Well, said Marrowbone, this was what I must do. Beneath Newbury's, at Meadowsweet, as I must well know, there lay a little cove, or inlet. Thither he would come to me in a vessel, when he had news from Nayle, which would be soon. I, meanwhile, must bring down the 'scaped slaves from out the hills, as many as could be, tho' still keep them hidden close to Meadowsweet; whom he would come and carry off by night, and I too, if we were all brave and vigilant.

This seemed to me a fine plot as much for our enlistment on any pirate ship, as for the easier capture of all of us were Marrowbone a traitor, seeking government gold. But he, peering at me, read my thoughts, and laughing, said, 'Boy, this island is no place where any scheme of betterment to a slave may stand unfraught with danger. It must be, then, for you and your friends to judge of which danger to your lives is greater: to die hunted in the hills, or risk death in a manly endeavour to escape it.'

This sounded candid enough, and yet I said to him, 'True,

Marrowbone; but my friends will surely wonder why you should seek to do them all these dangerous favours.'

'Ah, as to that,' said he, 'the answer is simple, and should reassure you. For each volunteer I bring to Captain Nayle, if the man be desperate and sturdy, Mr Nayle presents me with some golden guineas.'

To this I could only answer that I would send his message to my friends; and that if they agreed, I would ask them to come down as soon as I learned his boat, and he, could come to Meadowsweet.

So intent was I on all this plotting, that I did not notice Horatio was off the craft and, finding the horses guarded by another, had come striding up on me. I grovelled before him, beseeching his forgiveness, and saying (saving his pardon) I was seeking for some tobacco; but to my surprise he made no answer, but called on me to follow him alone up to the sea end of the mole.

There he turned to me and said (swaying his cane gently), 'Boy, Miss Diana, I am pleased to say, speaks well of you, and vows that, though but a lad, you are a worthy, sensible fellow.'

'I am her true servant, sir,' said I, little trusting this fair change of face.

'Aye – so I hope, and verily believe. Now, hearken to me, boy. It is Miss Diana's intent, ere long, to make an excursion, in my company and under my protection, on that vessel you see there; our course set to a neighbour island, that is some days' sail off. For the young lady has never left St Laughter, and sighs to peer over the horizon.'

I said no word to all this fibbing bombast, but stood meek, attentive and, I confess, mightily curious.

'But,' he continued, 'it could happen that her father, Mr Newbury, that worthy excellent gentleman, would not wish of this. For, as you may know, he cherishes his only daughter like a precious stone; and fears foolishly that, bereft of his constant care and vigilance, some rare evil might befall her.'

'But sir,' said I candidly. 'In sure care such as yours, how could that be?'

He eyed me, half frown'd, then gave me his snake's smile. 'Well said, boy, and true. Now, Miss Diana counts on more than your obedience – on your discretion. And when she is ready to make this small voyage, you will carry her first here to Joie.'

'But sir!' cried I. 'For this, when he discovers it, Mr Newbury will flay off all my skin!'

'Nay, lad – for consider!' He drop't his voice. 'You will travel with us, lad, on this fair excursion! And when we sail back here to St Laughter, she and I, we shall leave you on the island we are visiting richer by a loaded purse, and spread it around that you have 'scaped. As indeed, you will have.'

('Aye,' thought I. 'The purse a stone round my neck, and my haven the Caribbean sea.')

'Bless you, Mr Horatio!' I exclaimed. 'I know Miss Diana wishes me well, and I have equal confidence in your benevolence.'

At this he swore me to secrecy, with also the gentle threat of my tenderest members being slic'd should I betray them; and turning, he strode back ahead of me to the horses, where Miss Diana was awaiting our return.

On the ride back, after Horatio had turned aside at Valentine, she grew silent, breaking only into a fury when I lagged; and at last, in the barren patch at the north end of the island (I mean, where fewer plantations are), she did me a favour unknown, almost, to a slave, which was to let me ride upon the horse's rump behind her; though I was not, she said, to place my arms about her waist, but cling on to the saddle; and this condescension might also have been due to her anxiety of getting back to Meadowsweet, before night fall, when her absence would be surely noted.

But she enjoyed the fortune of the brave (some say the wicked), for our return was not specially remark'd. As for me, tho' I was then a sturdy lad, I was so wreck'd by all this running in bare feet on rocks as to be made into half a corpse. So that when my Master sent for me, I could hardly stagger to his room; though I tried hard to look alert, lest he should ask the cause of my exhaustion.

All he said to me, when I stood before him, was, 'I suppose, boy, that tho' you are no nephew to Mr Zachary, you can, like that worthy person, read?' And without waiting for a reply, he tossed a letter to me, which was as follows:

'Esteemed Sir,

The person concerning whom you write to me, calling himself Alexander Nairn, and purporting to be my nephew, is not of my blood, nor connected to any of my family; but he is indeed known to me, to my misfortune, as he is to my fellow magistrates here in Mortar, for a notorious liar, thief and rebel to his King and Government.

'This malefactor came to us some while ago in Mortar laying claim to being my dear dead sister's son; which unlucky youth, as we have since sadly discover'd, was slain in the recent disturbances in the Highlands. Aware of this death before we were, the wretch you hold prisoner determined wickedly to impersonate him; and at first half convinced us, since he seemed familiar with so many particulars (of our family, and so forth) which my dead nephew alone could know. But we soon grew to suspect that this imposter must have learn'd what he did through an acquaintance with my true nephew before his death; so that, having worm'd secrets and confidences from my poor relative (and then, for all we know, he being a traitor Highlander, turn'd into his executioner), this fraudulent criminal decided to simulate his victim; which he might have hop'd to do because my late nephew, being born in the Highlands and never coming South, was, save as a cherished name, unknown to us.

'How you should dispose of a creature so bereft of honesty and pity, you must be best judge. Here in Mortar, besides his plot to steal my nephew's name and property, he stole amply in the cruder form of goods; on our discovery of which, we first suspected the truth of his larger claim. Our magistrates confin'd him, but he escaped from Mortar, by a drunken guard (since himself imprison'd), to we knew not whither, until your communication came here to enlighten us.

'Your last consignment of molasses, Esteemed Sir, gave us much satisfaction here; though truth compels me to advise that with the greater calm descending on our distracted country now the rebellion is quite squash'd, the prices of all wares are falling from those frantick heights of which the revolt was the temporary impulsion; but of this more when you will receive, as you shortly shall, the full account of our Remittances for the cargo to your Bankers in the South, in London.'

'Well?' said Mr Newbury, when my eyes (with tears in them now) rose to meet his after reading this sentence to my surviving hopes.

'Sir, I can but say I have spoken truth to you, and my uncle has written one vast lie.'

'No doubt,' said Mr Newbury pleasantly. 'But this uncle who says he is not, is well known to me; and you, Mr Alexander Nairn (this he emphasised), are not known to me at all.'

'Sir, I am in your hands.'

'Indeed,' said he. 'And these hands will consign you, on the morrow, out of this house into the plantations, where you will learn what slavery really is; with a preface to your history of a hundred lashes, not for your crimes, but that you lied to me, and under oath. Be off with you now to your hut; pray for your survival, and thank Mr John Knox he has not—not yet, at any rate – predestined you to the hanging that your sins deserve!'

I bowed my head miserably, and withdrew. Out in the yard, I dash'd my eyes round about, then crouch'd like a startled whippet, I rac'd up into the hills.

The Hounds

HAD I stopp'd to think, after all day running in and out of Joie, how I could go even one step further, and this up mountain crags through jungle, I would have stayed riven fast; but luckily, I found the strength bestowed on weariest limbs by panic, and an empty mind. I tore up the peaks as in a nightmare: cut, tumbling, knock'd, and spurr'd on by my pains; and when I stopp'd, already a mile off, it was not that the fear was less, but my legs tottered under me, like brittle sticks.

Panting and gasping, my heart a cruel hammer, and trembling in sweat, I tried to hold back my fear and think. Against me were my solitude, no weapon, no food, and the certainty of bloodhounds on my track at the first light; and to help me, that somewhere in these summits there might be friends, though I could not be certain till I found out who they were.

All I could think to do was to keep on; to cross water often to trick the dogs; and once out of range of Meadowsweet, to start calling. For though this might bring me death if the 'scaped slaves wished me ill, the same death would come otherwise by hounds' fangs or starvation.

So I track'd a torrent by its echo, and clambered up its middle, avoiding even to step upon the stones. And perhaps to aid me since it might wash off any scent, the heavens opened and it rained heavily, with thunder. At first dawn it cleared, and I paused on a summit to make an assessment.

I was some miles above Meadowsweet, which I could just descry; but as to the peak my feet had carried me to, they had not chosen happily. For I saw it was an isolated cone – that is, did not connect onto the general chain; to reach which, I would first have to go down again, before once more climbing up. The discouragement of this discovery was augmented by the first distant carolling of the hounds; which was not their ordinary yelping, horrible enough, but the hysterick gulpings of a promise to them of blood. And I thought, at this moment, of their feverish snufflings at my cot for the sweet scent of their prey.

Well, I could yell too, and I began calling my miseries to the dawn; but still fearing to be heard far beneath, I kept my note low, and tried to imitate a bird. All that came answering was a wet silence, dripping and forlorn; and such a loneliness upon that drenched mountain, it will not be believed, but I yearned with a pang for the company even of the slave hut.

I thought that, being too weak now to try to make off down the mountain, I should best climb a tree. And as I looked at all those hundreds, to pick one from their similarity, I heard a voice that was not answer to any prayer; which beckoned me towards one half in water, whose branches I could grip without touching any soil, and I started climbing up. I scream'd when a hand gripped mine and yank'd me into a solid fork. I lashed out (imagining a jaguar, if not a spirit) when a voice said, 'Now, now . . .' and it was Joalla. I clutch'd at him weeping, till he handed me a bap which I grabb'd, and lit me a pipe; which caused me to grow calmer, and more comforted. For tho' our state was still perilous enough, the tree seemed to me like a castle.

'What now?' I asked at last.

'We wait the dogs; but perhaps they will not come.'

'The men?'

'Too far below: they will not be here yet.'

'Why did you not come out and look for me?'

'To be sure you were alone.'

'Oh, I am not trusted!' He was silent. 'Joalla. How did you know which tree I would come to?'

'How? Magic. Keep still, now.'

And so, stuck drenched on the tree fork, I wondered. Magic, we know exists of certainty when it is sacred; for miracles of Our Lord are proof of this. Men, too, make miracles, for we are told the saints did, and this to be one reason they are sanctified. But a puzzlement arises. A Christian is forbidden magic which, unless sacred, is of the devil. But those same saints who made miracles were not saints when they did. Were their deeds, then, sinful during life, and holy after death when they themselves were made holy?

And what of all other magic, which is Satan's? Of a truth, the Church believes in it; I mean, believes that it exists, for we burn witches. But how can we be sure? I know that in the Highlands, however devout they are, they all credit sorcery which the Church (even Papist) does not countenance. My Father believed in Second Sight implicitly, and would trust a fey word as firmly as any Priest's; yet I cannot believe him evil, or his countrymen.

And where the blessed light of the Gospels has not fallen? Is all their magic a damnation? If so, and Joalla spoke true, he had saved my body by the payment of his soul; and mine too. Yet I was grateful for the tree, and the spell that brought me there.

Then came the bay and scruffle of the hounds.

Joalla took, from a stout twig among the foliage, a bow and four arrows, which he slid between his fingers. When they crash'd yowling and slobbering below us, he let fly fast, and two kicked up screaming, which their fellows leap't on to devour. 'Come,' said Joalla, and he started down the tree.

'Those still alive will not follow us?'

'The arrows are venom'd. Come.'

'But the men.'

'Come, boy! The men are a mile back down the hill.'

As soon as we touched ground, Joalla led off at a trot, but to my surprise I was all fervour. And then the thought came to me that the pipe he had given me tasted strange, and I wondered if it could have held one of those potients I have heard the Caribes are famous for. We slithered down the crags on the far side, crossed a fair river, and started up the further mountain which was steeper. Though we halted at times to listen, there was no sound of pursuit.

We climbed all day, and now I could understand what, from the coast, seemed hard to: that escaped slaves found a refuge here. From below, all looks exquisite and easy; but on these wilds, a whole regiment would be lost. In the Highlands, with all Stinking Billy's redcoats, hundreds of the Clansmen remained hidden; but in St Laughter, was only a Company of men; and if the island be small, its landscape is far wilder, besides hotter.

At length we reached the foot of a furrow'd precipice, rising some hundred feet, and curving outward. Here Joalla took out a flute and played a short shrill melody. After a pause, a rope of tendrils weighted by a stone, came over, and he brac'd it round me, then blew a single note. At once I was hoisted up, and tho' I was cut on juts, and swang and spun to make me dizzy, I was heaved safe on to the top.

There were four men, all Caribes I thought, who said nothing to me, but set about raising my companion. So I spied around, and saw I was on the edge of a small plateau, undulating and not so thickly wooded as the slopes below. In the distance was what looked to be a village, and I thought I discern'd figures moving there. Up here, the air was also lighter.

When Joalla was hoisted, and he had taken a last survey of the valley, we set off (just as travellers have told us) in an Indian file; tho' I, ragged and cut, was a sorry Indian among these originals. We entered a thick clump, and pursuing a labyrinth of narrow paths that circled till I lost all feeling of direction (the sun not aiding, for the boughs hid it quite off), we came into a clearing with palm huts, from which there stepp'd men, grasping weapons. 'Blood seed, look who ear,' said Archibald.

The Fugitives

AFTER a day for my recovery, I learned from Archibald of the outlaw republic of St Laughter; for such one could call it, since the writ of King George scarcely extended to these heights.

Its rulers were the Caribes; and how many of these survived in all St Laughter, he was not sure. He had seen six of them here, but guessed there might be more on other peaks whom those in his camp knew, but would not speak of; and there must be women somewhere, for all the Caribes were young. Perhaps this was a chief reason for their silence.

The escaped slaves were now eighteen up here, though the number rose and fell with arrivals, or with deaths and captures. But over this majority, the Caribes kept easy dominion; for they had weapons, could find food, and knew the country. So far as he knew, the Caribes had not killed any slave, except when, by fear or jealousy, they were attacked. The real enemy of the slaves (besides the whites) was sickness, for many died of fevers that seemed not to afflict the Caribes at all.

Then why did they preserve the slaves or, at least, allow of their existence? Archibald was not sure he knew the answer. The slaves brought nothing with them and, once arrived, performed no useful service; and besides, the Caribes scarcely hid their contempt for them, or for anyone in the wide world not born to their lost and abandoned tribe. The only reason Archibald could think of for their toleration was that the escaped slaves were an irritation to the robbers who had seized upon their island.

'You fortunate, you know,' said he, 'they jus' not slit you pink troat at first sight of you.'

'For that, it seems I must thank Daniel. Yet if they love you little more than they do us, why did Joalla carry his message to me?'

Archibald nodded sagely. 'That because he the only slave they lissen to. And why they lissen to he, is that they like he *obeah*; also the sweet plans he imagine up.'

'One of which, I hear, is to kidnap Newbury's daughter, who has six armed overseers and twelve mastiffs to guard her, beside her father.'

'Yeah – sweet plan. But you see, if we get she, we strike a big bargain, so Daniel tink.'

'If we get her. And if they keep the bargain.'

'Yeah. Well, you better speak to Daniel when he finish he mornin' prayers. He the brain man up ear. I jus' the comedian.'

'And where is Alfonso?'

'Boy! Does he make our hearts flutter! You know what he do? Take you: you get away from Meadowsweet, you want to go peeping back there? I tink not. But Alfonso, he must be tiger: show brave. And what he do? He pop back down to Trenoggin place, lookin' for rum an' ting.'

'And he got back?'

'Oh yeah – but no rum. Pistol, though, he find hide. Two day now he out again on some other valiant expedition.'

'He has encountered no soldiers?'

'He say no: tho' from time to time they come up, seeking. But not up far – too high, too hot, jungle too fierce. Beside, we hear them easy, oathin' and clatterin', an' night time, they jus' don't try.'

'And Daniel has some wild plan to combat them?'

'Better ask he: he the general.'

We found Daniel seated in a hut, entranc'd, and were frowned to wait the conclusions of his parley with the sable deities. At length he emerged, and greeted me with a strange welcome: 'Well, you know now we could kill you nice an' easy.'

'Not if you want to get off this island, as you say.'

'You got like a plan for that?'

'I think a good one.'

'Speak.'

I told him as much about Marrowbone and his proposal as might entice him, but not enough to let him bring the affair himself to any conclusion. He noticed this and said, 'You not tell we who this man is, who talk to you of Mr Pirate?'

'No.'

'An' you not goin' to?'

'Later.'

'I see – you make condition. Now, you hear about how we goin' to capture this Diana?'

'I hear about how you want to. But you know she is guarded, and since my escape, there may be soldiers at Meadowsweet.'

'No matter, we must grab she.'

'But why? Our chance of getting off to join with Nayle is slender. What will be left of it if we stir them all up with such a ravishment? An adventure that may lead to our own deaths?'

'We get the girl,' he said. 'When we get she, they cannot kill us. She too precious to them.'

'To Newbury. To the soldiers, do you think? What do they care?'

'The soldiers are *nothing* on the island. Only the planters. You were not born here, remember.'

'As you say, Daniel. You get her: and then? They will let you sail away before you hand her over? Or you will hand her over, and will they let you sail away?'

'I tink you stupid. Of course we not hand her over.'

'Oh. So what do we do with her?'

'Who know? Give her to the Caribes to hold. Or maybe keep her for bargain with Mistah Nayle.'

'Then they will never let you off the island! You will bring a whole regiment here from Resurrection to hunt you down.'

'Not if we act clever. Now, then. Who at Meadowsweet can we trust?'

What made it hard, nay impossible, to reason with Daniel, was that he proceeded not by logic, but faith. He dwelt in certainties! This gave him a force beyond all doubt, but did not encourage doubters.

'I can see only two,' I answered. 'Bandele, an African, and Priscilla.'

'Who this Bandele?'

'A slave brought here with us on *Providence*.' He listened absently, and said, 'So Priscilla she down there?'

'Yes. But she cannot do much to help us now.'

'Who say so?'

'The girl is with child.'

'Oh? Who make she so? Who? Was you? Now, you lissen to me, Bukra boy. You leave black woman alone – you see? You want your troat cut?'

'Easy, man,' said Archibald.

'This blood clot slave think he planter man.'

'Hé, Daniel, maybe the girl like he.'

'Like *he*? Do not you mamagai me, Archibald. He less than nuttin. He better keep off mixin' skin.'

'And you, Daniel?' cried I. 'To seize upon Diana: what is that really for? To help you to escape? Or is that to "mix skin"?'

'You tink *that* why I want her?'

'And not by free choice, as I with Priscilla, but by theft!'

He jumped at me, but Archibald stood between us. I confess I was afraid of Daniel — I mean not just of my lonely posture there among them, but of the power of his malevolence. But I put as bold a face on as I was able, and said,

'I shall not argue with you about what may now be nothing. Diana Newbury will soon be on the high seas, if she is not already.'

This caused a babble and enquiry, and I told them of her plot of elopement with Horatio. Daniel looked darker, reflected a moment, then cried, 'That fix it, then! Archibald, go hunt up Alfonso! We make that snatch of she tonight.'

Well, let them make it! I decided. For was not my own chance of escape better if I tried to make my way alone to Marrowbone, and so join Nayle? But then, would Marrowbone, with his love of guineas, take me alone in a perilous journey across the sea? No, he would not: he would want many slaves to offer Nayle. My lot was cast with Daniel, for good or evil.

What was more, I knew I could not escape alone. Not that this was impossible, if I had the will to match good fortune: in an enterprise so hazardous, to be alone might be less dangerous. But I could bear solitude no more. And though I mistrusted Daniel (for he let me see clearly enough I ought to), I had a kind of bleak faith in his dark star; at all events, in his far greater capacity for action, come what may.

Alfonso did not return till night, when I was sleeping. Of what they plotted without me, I can but guess; so that whether they might have left at once were Alfonso rested, I do not know. Or perhaps they decided to include me in their plan because of my familiarity with Marrowbone, and their greater hope, through me, of taking ship. So the start was fixed for the next night, and I was called into counsel in the early morning.

Daniel had decided we must descend not on Meadowsweet, but Valentine; on Horatio's lair, not Diana's father's. For this his reason was that it was nearer the bay, and boats, and at Meadowsweet, since my escape, they would be the more alerted. To the objection of more overseers at Valentine, and soldiers nearer in Joie, the answer was that there we would be least expected: ever the bold general's plan, which may flourish when the enemy do not have the same wise thought.

I said I admitted their boldness (while trembling at it inwardly), but that a chief objection to it, if to seize Diana was really an essential, was that she might not come at all to Valentine, or that she had already come and gone. This doubt I cast, though, with a scant conviction: for while I wished her to escape them, I also hankered for her ravishment. My words impressed nobody; for Daniel, casting on me a disdainful glare, said, 'She *not* gone, she *will* come by this Horatio. An' that when we wait for her and catch she.'

'Magic tells you so?'

'Women tell me, boy. She hot for that fellow, an' he not dare no more to go by Meadowsweet.'

So it was ordained we should set out in time to reach the heights over Valentine by nightfall. Joalla was away, but another Caribe would guide us thither. Our arsenal for this enterprise consisted, beside knives that all of us now had, in Alfonso's pistol with no flint, powder or ball, and a venom'd spear Joalla had given me which, so much we all feared its accidental prick, we decided to leave behind. We all carried smoked snake, Daniel bearing thoughtfully an extra ration for his captive.

Our project seemed such a folly (at least to me, and I believe even to Archibald with his blind faith) that it gave us all a kind of special resolution. There is also to be remembered the goad of desperation and, for the slaves, of hatred. A slave does not deem his life less precious than any other's; but he will stake it more readily on a frantic hazard, because escape offers him the most precious prize.

When we were muster'd we found ourselves delayed by propitiary prayers of Daniel's; but I could not profit by this pause to make any to a cleaner faith, since I had sullied it, or meant to, which scripture teaches us to be the same. Our two companions passed their time in temporal matters, sharpening knives. The Caribe waited motionless on one foot, the other resting across his knee.

The Escape

WE WERE up over Valentine at dusk, and the excitement of our target lying below was match'd by a huge alarm at the effrontery of our intent. And at this moment I must needs to admire the calm resolve of Daniel, who peered out on his battle-field with the assurance of a very Marlboro. I could see the advantage to the general of choosing night: not only for its dark, but because the slaves would be lock'd in (making fewer eyes), the overseers mostly besotten, and the dogs sleepier. But the obstacle was that I could not suppose Diana, if she kept a tryst, would travel about the wild roads of St Laughter other than by day, even upon a secret mission.

But Daniel had guessed better than I. For he mutter'd, 'Yes, it there!'

'What?'

'She horse. I know he. I see that horse when she trot along to Joie.'

'You think she is in the house already?'

'She there, I tell you. Later tonight they ride down to the boat together.' He turned to me. 'Now listen, boy. When she come over here from Meadowsweet, she must come with a slave. An' she not have that slave lock in because she need to take him with her when she flit. So here what you do. You know all the slave on Meadowsweet. You pop down and find which he be. If he like sensible, then you bring him up to talk with we.'

'And if he is not? Or if it be an overseer?'

'Be no overseer, being she must move in secret. You go down discover. Quick, now, boy!'

To be chosen for a hazardous task, and in front of witnesses, brings courage to the faintest hearted. I set off down hill, fearing, as I drew nearer to the plantation, the dogs (I mean their yelps, for they were chain'd) more than I did the men. I knew Valentine well, and where the stables were; so I circled round, fairly secure I would not be discover'd; for such is the despotism of St Laughter, that, save in Joie (where there are dissolute mariners), there are few marauders prowling outside, and thus few guards.

The sniff of dung and a faint whinneying told me I was close on my objective, and I clamber'd over the larva wall into hard arms that wrapp'd me, while a voice said, 'Bo-bo, why do you not use the gate?"

'Release me, Bandele!' cried I.

'I shall not do so till you promise you make no more noise. Countryman, I hear you thunder whole way down that mountain.'

I had scant time to bandy words with the garrulous African, and swiftly unfolded to him the dire project on which we were embark'd. He listened carefully, then said to me, 'But bo-bo, I do not think I need come up to your companion. Is bettah you all go down some mile along the way to Joie.'

'How so?'

'Ah! I think they leave soon, and if I am not here it seem suspicious.'

'True. And how shall we set upon them? Will they take guards?'

'Oh, no. Just Mistah Horatio and the young lady, I suppose.'

'And he on a horse with sword and pistols! How can we throw him?'

Bandele laughed. 'Will not be needed, countryman.'

'How so?'

'Because tonight I keep my promise to Mr Newbury. Yes. Tonight, bo-bo, Mistah Horatio will greet his ancestor.'

'Why?'

'Is magic, sah.'

I was enrag'd. 'Bandele!' cried I. 'This is no time for confidence in witchcraft.'

'Oh no? Well, perhaps I can say there is also a pin upon his saddle, with a danger point. Come!' He took my hand, and led me to the stables. Pointing to Horatio's steed, he said, 'Please do not touch, but on his saddle there is fix a bramble.'

'Why?'

Bandele grew peevish. 'Listen, bo-bo,' said he. 'I kill him with my magic, certainly. But to make more sure, I use a little spikey plant I know of that have a special action.'

'The moment he feels it, he will brush it off.'

'Will be too late. Or perhaps he think is a mosquito.'

Time seemed too short for further parley with this dubious ally. 'But Bandele,' said I. 'If you do this for Mr Newbury, will you not wish to return and claim your reward?'

'No sah, because he not give me any, but try kill me to keep his secret. No, I think I shall like to join with you expedition.'

Seizing the good fellow's hand, I said we would be stationed along the road within an hour; and that he must, on some pre-text about the horses, delay his masters till we were well postured. Then I set off up the mountain, but the journey was not so far, for the conspirators had come half-way down the hill, and spied my climb. Daniel expressed approval, save that he had no trust in the African's spells.

'We must go catch them,' said he 'where the road cross the stream, and they have to walk their horses. He will come first, see. We leap on the woman horse, me and Alfonso, and you two pounce on the man and chop he off.'

Ere long we were positioned on each side of the burn. The huge night was silent, save for the sea and a complaint of crickets. We strained our ears for hoof-beats, clutching our knives.

But they rode on the grass verge for secrecy, and came out on us suddenly. And what struck us dumb was that there were three figures on horseback, beside the running slave. And the leader, I saw at once to my dismay, was one of the fiercest in St Laughter: it was Mr George.

'A quick drink for the horses, Mr Wilson, sir,' said he.

'Hasten on, George. We must not delay,' replied the Planter on whom (unless he were a spectre) the spells cast by Bandele had as yet no dire effect.

'And the gift, sir, the gift,' said George. 'You will remember?'

'As I promised to you, George; and as you did to me your silence.'

'Horatio, what halts us?' came Diana's voice from further up the slope.

'The stream, sweetheart, we are crossing now. Come up betwixt us, angel.'

A blood-curdling shriek (proceeding from Bandele) split the still air, and in an instant all was violent disarray. George cried, 'Death, slaves!', fir'd his pistol through Archibald's face (who dropt like a stone into the flood), and by Alfonso was stabbed in the back, and hack'd off his horse to death. Horatio's steed rear'd, and he fell on the rocks stunn'd. The girl was snatch'd off by Bandele, Daniel aiding. All this in a minute, then silence fell save for panting, a last groan from George, and the girl's scream muffled up.

Daniel fell to berating Bandele. 'Bind her, mask her,' he cried, 'but we keep her virgin.'

'Bo-bo, what are you telling me? No woman is virgin in St Laughter.'

'Leave her, or take this cut.'

'Peace, countryman. I just hold her for you.'

Alfonso lifted up Horatio, and smiled to see he was alive. He proceeded slowly with his knife, amid horrid screams, and throwing parts, one by one, over his shoulder.

'Just stab, man!' cried Daniel. 'They hear that scream off in Joie!'

I could hear and see no more, and went to gather in the horses. The corpse of George, and the remainder part of Horatio, were now stow'd beneath the rocks. Daniel was kneeling beside Archibald, praying. He rose saying, 'That one boy not see the day break,' and pulled his friend's body to the shadows. The girl lay like a bundle by the river, limbs fetter'd, sight and sound bandaged up. Bandele crouched beside her, but a short way off.

An argument arose about the horses; to take them, or go on foot? Daniel said two should walk and others ride them, seeming there were guardians to the girl. At this lunatick plan I quite revolted, and said no, let me go alone to Joie, seek out Marrowbone, and come with him in his boat round to where the stream joined up with the sea. If I could not find

Marrowbone, or he refused, we had time, before dawn, to get up to the hills.

Daniel was discontented and mistrustful of my whim, believing he could make some capture of a boat in Joie; but the others for once thought this was madness, and he was overruled. 'Well,' Daniel said, 'you not do much to fight the battle, so perhaps you could be useful now.' This being agreed, with much ill humour and mistrust, I set off lightheaded down the road.

Perhaps a true warrior feels, at death, no kind of sorrow, since he offers freely of his own; but I was heavy at the thought of these three corpses. Even for cruel treachery, death seemed too big a price for foolish Horatio to pay! Far more than he was worth, it being so tremendous and he so paltry! And Archibald, poor clown, that was born for happiness, and easy jokes. For Mr George I felt less sorrow; for I believed that only he could have understood his death.

As for the girl, I felt the only injustice of her fate lay in her ignorance, nurtured like a tropick flower in Meadowsweet since she was born. How could these planter brats ever be wise, or good? How could they invite anything but greed of their equals, hatred of those they ruled? And how could they, even, ever understand their destinies?

And so I came in to Joie, and crept down about the mole. Nothing stirr'd, and the boats lapp'd soft taps on the quay: looking so small, although so graceful, these little chests that climb mountains of the sea! On Marrowbone's skiff there was a lanthorn . . . but was he there? Or others? I climbed the mole wall, and threw shells against the hull. A voice cried, 'I have pistols!', and I called his name. 'Come out, boy,' he said, appearing on the deck, armed as he had warned.

But not yet. 'I have three 'scaped slaves for you,' said I.

'Three beside you?'

'Aye.'

''Tis little, boy. Scarce worth the voyage. Where?'

'Hid: not far away, but they cannot tarry.'

'Stout lads?'

'None stouter. We have a hostage, too.'

'A hostage?'

'Aye: a woman.'

'I want no slave-girls.'

'No, a white.'

'Which?'

'Planter's child.'

'Which, boy?'

'From Meadowsweet.'

There was a silence. Then he said, 'You lie.'

'Not I.'

''Tis not possible.'

'She is there: there with the slaves.

'Living?'

'Alive.'

'Not ravished?'

'Nay.'

'Boy! Were that true, for Nayle it **were a** ransom!'

'So I fancied.'

'And for me.'

'Also.'

'But you deceive me, boy.'

'Mr Marrowbone!' cried I. 'You **can** never know that till you come and see. But you must **hasten: soon** it will be dawn.'

'I need stores.'

'Fetch them.'

'Show yourself, boy. I will not shoot you . . .'

'Nor betray me?'

'God's life! Here!' And he threw his pistol onto the mole. I leapt over and seiz'd it, and he came on land. 'Boy,' he said, 'I believe you. Tarry on board, keep hid.'

We were away in an hour, smoothly into the bay, then veer'd round northward. Marrowbone asked me for particulars, and I told him what seemed needful. But he was mostly silent with thoughts I could partly guess, and one soon broke out of his mouth.

'I think of pursuit,' he said. 'Tell me: what is there to prove that you men stole the girl from Horatio Wilson?'

'On Daniel and Alfonso, nothing, except that all 'scaped slaves are suspect. On myself more, for I fled from Meadowsweet. On Bandele most, when they find she and he gone in the morning.'

'Aye, the African,' said he. 'And how long to find the corpses?'

'It will be soon: dogs, stench, flies . . .'

'Aye. And Marrowbone's boat was out: you see my drift?'

'I see your profit also, Marrowbone.'

'True. But to take 'scaped slaves is little, for few care. Go carry away a planter's daughter . . . Well, Nayle is an honest villain, and will be generous. And I, I shall stay away from St Laughter for a spell. The Caribbean is vast, boy, deck'd with a thousand islands!'

Soon we tack'd in to shore, for Marrowbone knew where the stream fell into the ocean. But he would not come in to land until I had waded to find my friends, and signal all was well. I tried to persuade him, fearing the sea creatures, but he yielded not. So muttering a prayer, I slipp'd in the sea and staggered to the land.

I found them smoking, and was glad to join in this relaxation. They listened to me, and Daniel said, 'He is to be trust?'

'Yes. He risks his life on this.'

'No, not that . . . What if he sell we to this pirate?'

'What can we do? If the pirate finds us worthy, he will take us. If not, kill us anyway. We have no other choice, and dawn is coming.'

'Let we go then – call the man boat in. But all understand now. The woman can be whip, but I slice any one who try to take she. She the only treasure we can trade with to this pirate.'

'He can just seize her, as we did.'

'No, cos we hide her first, and make like bargain.'

'You trustful, bo-bo,' said Bandele.

The Cay

WHEN the Dons sailed into the Caribbean, on their terrible adventure, they soon found the monster islands. As the ships flock'd, and their domain extended over the huge sea, they happened on smaller places; as does a monarch, first gazing at his diamonds, spy the pearls. But hundreds of minute island gems remained; and even today, when our navies and those of France and the Low Countries have joined, to their dismay, the fleets of Spain and Portugal, great tracts of these seas remain uncharted. For the nations are so gutted with the riches of the larger islands, that the smallest are left solitary to the wild birds, the shipwrecked, the castaway, and the buccaneers.

So Marrowbone explained to me as we spun over the ocean, St Laughter at first a dot, then far behind. His landfall, he told me, would be a Cay, or small island where there was not even a Caribe; but a fair anchorage, and fresh water. So this was a cherished spot for Nayle and his confederates, to put in for rest, flight, or a careen. Perhaps Nayle would not be there, indeed probably; but it was his habit to leave small parties on the Cay (sometimes for punishment), and they would have some news of the Captain's course.

Captain Nayle, he assured me, was a gallant and honourable man; indeed, Marrowbone half persuaded me we were to meet some Drake or Frobisher. For in the Caribbean, he declared, two writs ran: those of the warring European nations and those, lighter but of some consequence, of the pirate chieftains; and of all these Nayle, if not the most considerable, was the most respected.

And what of our conduct to him? Here, Marrowbone replied, he must speak roundly with me. If Nayle misliked us, our throats would instantly be slit; or perhaps we might serve for the frolic of walking the plank, or keel-hauling. And even if he accepted us, we must understand he would at all times have absolute powers of death over us, and be very apt to use them. But if he took a fancy to us, and we serv'd him well, our merits would be our protection; for even a pirate needs a crew, and cannot, said Marrowbone, split everybody's gut. As to the virtues Nayle would expect of us, resolute strength, utter villainy, and total obedience were the prime ones; though any accessory skills (as mine, he said, of some modest seamanship), would be of merit.

Mostly, my mentor said, we must well understand that to be a pirate is as to be a slave: that is, an absolute condition, from which it is almost impossible to escape. True, elderly pirates, if well trusted, were sometimes permitted to retire, as was Trenoggin. But as to the younger, they were not only outlaws to the authorities, but such was the fear among their comrades of any treachery, that they would be watch'd closely for the least spark of disloyalty by their fellow buccaneers.

'You have, lad,' he said, 'though young, good training for this enterprise that Nayle may fancy: I mean you have been press-ganged and enslaved, and Nayle likes men of youthful desperation.'

'Let us hope he admires my comrades too,' said I.

'I doubt not he will. Yet in truth, boy, I have a large reserve about the African – not for his villainy, I mean, but that they in St Laughter might seek to pursue us if ever they caught him, and he betray us.' Marrowbone looked about him, then at the far horizon. 'Perchance,' said he, 'it might be well to send him swimming?'

'For what purpose, Marrowbone?'

'I mean, among the sharks.'

'God forbid! You must not think of it.'

'Aye . . . perhaps not. Mayhap all will be well.'

To turn his mind from such fell thoughts, I said how Mr Trenoggin had declared to me that pirates sometimes assisted their legitimate governments; and was this so? True, Marrowbone rejoined; but this was a matter so delicate and complex that he did not believe that, at this stage of my apprenticeship, I should trouble my young head about it.

Stuff'd with this wisdom, I retir'd to the prow to smoke, and gaze out on the sparkling ocean. My intent, rash and presumptuous as it seem'd, was quite the opposite of that enjoined on me by Marrowbone: namely, that I would seek to use the pirates both to escape out of the West Indies, and from them. And then whither? I had a dream of the Americas; for I knew that, in the North-east part of them, were colonies of worthy and devout Calvinists and, indeed, fellow Scots. Thither I would struggle, heaven willing, to build a new life after all these misfortunes and disasters.

Daniel joined me in the prow, and now seemed freer in his speech. Perhaps because we were well away with less anxiety, perhaps because I had not betray'd them as he feared, perhaps also (so I flatter'd myself) that he was beginning to divine I possess'd some youthful sagacity. Besides, this was the first day of his life outside St Laughter; and stern as our general was, he could not but be a little overaw'd.

'This Bandele,' he said, 'he a good spar, you know, but the Africans is wild: not tink.'

'You are jealous, Daniel, of his interest in your captive?'

'Me jealous of that pussy-tongue African? No, man. But he like act impulsive, not plan ahead.'

'The hot blood of your ancestors fires his veins.'

'Now, you not make joke, Bukra boy, or me sling you out the side.'

'Marrowbone thought of doing so to Bandele.'

'He do? Now tell me why?' I did so, and he said, 'This Mr Marrowbone have a nasty foolish thought: I better speak to he.'

'Alfonso has awoken yet?'

'Yes, boy. He jus' give that pussy-piece a lashin' till his arm tire.'

'I heard no sound . . .'

'Still gag. I better let she take a walk on deck, or she get sick an' lose her value.'

The kidnapp'd heiress, when she appeared, looked fearful, but I could see at once the spirit of the Newburys was not broken. For she walked on the prow like a chas'd cat which, though in acute alarm, still trusts its teeth and claws. She bade me good morning with a fair cordiality; that is, if no longer with the total arrogance of Meadowsweet, enough of it to show she still possess'd a power: which was, perhaps, that even in this extremity, she was one woman among five men, whose discord might present her with a weapon.

'So what do you intend to me, boy?' said she, half anxious, yet contemptuous as well. 'Is it death, violation, ransom, or all three?'

'Ransom.'

'Aye, money. Poor Horatio sought the same.'

'And you were willing.'

'I? Once escap'd from my father, and carried away to Europe, I would have laughed at him, and his pretensions to me and Meadowsweet!'

'You did not love him, then?'

She gave a romantick look, that seemed to me false, and said, 'He might have served, boy, for a husband .. But I have other dreams than to be mere mistress of two plantations on St Laughter.'

'Diana! You do not sorrow at his death?'

'Why,' she said, ''tis sad . . .'

She cried a little: but really, it seemed all fellow creatures were her toys! When she had ceas'd (mostly in sorrow for herself, it seemed), I said to her, 'Mr Newbury, at any rate, will be pleased you have escaped Horatio.'

She turned to me flushed and suddenly enraged. 'But not pleased at your pranks!' she cried. 'Believe me, boy, he shall have the whole navy on you!'

'He has such power?'

'Not he, but His Excellency. Once the Governor learns of this, do you think he will allow any Planter's child to be stolen away by slaves? And whipp'd! Slave, do you know *I* have been whipp'd?'

'Aye.' And I felt no sorrow for her.

'He will seek you out and punish you! His whole authority, and the planters', will pursue you to the end!'

'That may not help you . . .'

She looked round the boat, then back at me hard. 'Perchance not,' she said, 'but I have learned not to fear . . .' Now she began to look ingenious, and turning to me with the sweet

130

appeal of a winning child, she whisper'd, 'Boy! A fortune for you and the pilot if you slay the slaves and put back to St Laughter!'

'Miss Diana: even if I trusted you, which I shall never, I would not do it.'

'You do not love me, Alexander?'

'Aye.'

'And you will not do this?'

'No, Diana.'

'You fear to?'

'It is not only that I fear to . . .'

She flew into a blaze: 'Then enjoy the days left to you before hanging!'

Daniel returned and with some relish, and a horrid courtesy, told her to go below again and wash the cabin; whither, with a flounce and toss, she went. 'Hé, she try to bribe you, I expec',' he said.

'Yes.'

'An' you refuse: you saint, boy.'

'She will try Marrowbone, as well.'

'I know so. That is why we kill he. Also because he know too much of we.'

'And then what? Sail on with no charts?'

'Later, man. Is plenty time.'

I saw his glance. 'And I shall be next, Daniel?'

'Kill *you*, boy? Hé, you not trustin', are you. Beside, you a seaman. No Marrowbone, we need you on the tiller.'

The sun grew high, and Alfonso with Bandele took to fishing with lines offered them by Marrowbone. Alfonso was in high delight for never, he told us, had he been in a boat before; so strange it is that on tiny St Laughter, which is all sea, a child can grow on a plantation without even permission for a swim. Bandele, he of the Coast, was a great scientist at angling; but tho' he brandish'd the lines with much address, caught nothing.

'Blood seed,' cried Alfonso, 'this clot fish no want us in their yard. Havin' an old maas down the bottom there, an' not want no baccanale where we can get at they.'

'Perhaps they are not hungry,' said Bandele. 'Perhaps they are satisfy with one anothah.'

'Hé, that jus' like an African to tink they poor fish be cannibal, you know.'

'Oh-ho! So we eat ourselves in Africa?'

'Go – way! Everybody know you African boy *gobble* one another, don't tell me no.'

There was a shrill cry from the stern, and I ran to it to see Marrowbone's head bobbing behind the stern, and his arm waving. Daniel was leaning over. 'He fall in,' he said.

I grasped the tiller to swing it round, but he held me hard. 'No, let we go on,' he said.

'But we cannot reach the Cay without him!'

'Yes, man: look! It there now right ahead!'

There was indeed a line on the horizon. 'But how do you know it *is* the Cay?' I cried.

'He tell me so.'

'Before you pushed him?' I said, much ashamed, and looking back.

'Let we not argue now. You the sailor – steer we into port.'

'But I know not the reefs, the rocks, the currents.'

'Boy, you get us there – I know!'

'Your magic tells you?'

132

'Well, it tell me Marrowbone would drown.'

I could think of no reply to that and, heart sinking, I set my course; doubly dismay'd because my skill as a mariner came from a fishing boat at Mortar, and washing slops upon the slaver. But the wind was set fair, the sea calm, and all I could do about the rocks was watch and hope. I looked back again for Marrowbone, but he had vanish'd.

Diana clamoured to come up again and was allowed, tho' still fetter'd. When she saw me at the helm, and no Marrowbone, her eyes narrow'd in a surprised fear, but then came an amused scorn as she looked at me, saying nothing. I gaz'd round anxiously for any sail, in fear both to find one, or that we were so alone. And what, I wondered, if there was no one on the Cay, and we with no Marrowbone to steer us to another island? Daniel, I thought, was a general who believed in burning boats; and so we sailed on.

Towards evening, we could see the reef and, as if by our general's magic, a clear break to the harbour. We sailed in, and saw no other boat. The Cay was a quarter mile ahead, and was perhaps four times as long. It was low and bare, save for one wooded hill towards which, thinking of water, I now steered.

As we drew closer we could see one single man upon the beach who, from this far, I thought to be white and of a medium age. As the sail flopp'd and we stood in, he waded out to pull us to the sand; and when we stepp'd onto the shore he said, as if unperturb'd to see us, 'I am Venison.'

'That is your name, sir?' I enquired.

'Yes: out of Delaware. You want water here, or have you lost your bearings?'

'We are hoping to meet a . . .'

'Hé,' Daniel interrupted. 'You alone on here?'

'There is but I,' quoth Venison.

'None hidden?'

'Take a look! You will find the stream up yonder, if you need it.'

He looked at us, seeming calm though wary, while Diana was taken out and seated upon the sand, and the three slaves, after gazing around cautiously, went off exploring, clutching at their knives. Mr Venison helped me beach the boat, then said, 'I guess it is Mr Nayle that you are looking for.'

'The same,' said I; and this was really the first moment when I fully believed that Nayle existed, so doubtful had I been of Marrowbone. I said to Venison, 'You know him, or where he may be found?'

Venison let out a laugh. 'I know him well enough, but I surely do not wish to know where he may be.'

When I coax'd a story from him, it chill'd my blood – that is, if it were exact, and by his tone it sounded so. Tho' 'tis true a colonist has so rude and prolonged an accent, that all his speech, whatever he may say, seems to have a truth in it.

Mr Venison was a seaman that, falling on evil days (in respect to which I did not too nearly press him), came upon Captain Nayle, and joined him in several Expeditions. On their last visit to the Cay (a month ago), the Captain had pick'd out a working party who, Venison perceiv'd, were all young and fresh to piracy. When Nayle told them to carry casks ashore, by night and none else watching, Venison suspected instantly that this was to bury treasure. But what he knew too, which the novices did not, was that on such occasions, the working party are all slain, so that the secret of the treasure shall stay hid.

Thus, as they labour'd with their burden, Nayle alone beside and armed, Venison suddenly sped off and, though fired at, hid himself by swimming to the reef and lying on the rocks there half submerg'd. More shots told him of his comrades' fate, and the sight of searchers round the island in the morning confirmed his certainty that Nayle sought to ferret him out. But the Captain was anxious to be off, and the ship sailed that afternoon; and what he fear'd now above anything, was the return of Nayle.

'And how did you live?' I asked. 'And indeed, how shall we?'

'Oh, the fish are plentiful and there are lines left a-plenty; and fire, too, for I have flints.'

'And the treasure,' I asked. 'You sought it out?'

Venison laugh'd. 'Boy,' he replied, 'I would not tell you if I knew of it; and if I did, and Nayle comes back, 'tis better for you that you should know nothing he can find by torture.'

'Aye,' said I. 'But you, Venison: what will you do when Nayle returns, for how can you hide from him once more if he searches for you hard and long?'

He made no reply at once to this, but asked for the tale of our adventures; which I in part told him feeling, I knew not why, some trust in him, and that I might find in him an ally.

Venison now glanced round, to make sure the others had not yet returned, and said, 'Boy, leave with me now! Nayle can do no good for you; and for me, he is an executioner! Besides, if he finds you here, he may well believe you have learned about the treasure.'

'But my friends wish to join with Nayle . . .'

'Then let them! Are they not 'scaped slaves? So what else

can they do? But you, boy! A fresh island, a fresh start, with me to steer you . . .'

'But they, left alone here on the Cay . . .'

'Lad, they can live like kings here! Fish, fruit, fresh water, till Nayle comes in for them.'

'But what of the girl?'

'We take her! Lad, 'tis our duty for she is white.'

'But she knows each of my secrets, and would certainly betray me.'

'Then let her stay here for whatever fate awaits her! But you and I must certainly escape!' And now, suddenly turned fierce, he gripp'd me by the throat and cried, ' 'Tis your last chance, boy! For if you do not come at once, I shall take your boat, and stab you if you seek to stop me! For what is my life if I linger on this Cay?'

By now our risen voices, and our tussle had caught the attention of Diana; and struggling to her feet, she stood as if hesitating, facing one way, and then that. Breaking away from Venison, I ran to her and seizing at her cried, 'Diana! You must 'scape with us, or you will die here and be ravish'd!' She stared at me, and at my wild earnestness that I believed then to be a fine resolve to save her, even if it brought me into danger.

But wrenching away from me, she cried out, repeating it, on Daniel! And from the bush I saw the Caribbeans and the African come running down brandishing their knives. Holding to her fast, and tearing her by the hair, I dragged her, legs trailing, towards the boat, which the American was already heaving in the surf. But now the three slaves had come upon us and tugged at her beside the waves, she shouting to them; and Venison leapt from the boat again and, reaching up at

Alfonso, planted his knife in the lad's neck, at which he fell gushing. His two friends stooped to save him, but the colonist seized on Diana, dragging her to the sea, and flinging her aboard all in a heap, she screaming out. I pushed the boat violently out, while the slaves, letting Alfonso fall (and he lay still), sprung into the sea after us in fierce pursuit. But it was too late; and my last glimpse of them was Daniel and Bandele trying vainly to raise their friend; and of Daniel looking up, and raising an arm at me of imprecation.

The Colonist

WE SET course to the north, for Venison said we could find islands there that were not British, but fiefs of the French king: places called by the Caribbeans 'France', for these specks they believe to be provinces of the Bourbon kingdom. As our nations were not now at war, he thought they would be friendly; at any rate, far more so than the islands ruled from Resurrection. In 'France', he said, we could safely leave our captive, for it would take her some time before she could persuade the French to restore her to St Laughter; and we, meanwhile, first selling our boat for sustenance, could try to take ship to the Americas.

Of the Americas he spoke with praise, tho' with a sort of contempt for the English mother that had nurtur'd them; and for this I said I could not reprove him, since we Scots, or many of us, believe England to be no mother, but a scourge. He told me that of all the colonies, Delaware was queen, and that I would be assur'd of a welcome there; but still my resolve was to go further north, among my people.

I was surprised to find in Venison a great remorse for the slaying of Alfonso; only our desperation, he declared, had forc'd him to it. For Venison (tho' he had slain him) spoke kindly of the slaves, saying that serfdom was an abomination to free men, corrupting their own liberties; and that he had always refused to serve himself on slavers. I asked was this sentiment general among the colonists, and here he sigh'd and owned that it was not, especially in the southern part, like Virginia.

'True,' said he, 'the Africks are barbarous, fit only for the humbler kind of task; but in time we may elevate them up, when their docile labour will need not fetters nor the lash.'

As for Diana, who stay'd weeping obstinately below, he said he thought her to be like all planters' daughters, that is, a pest. I thought he might have designs upon her virtue, but he seem'd an honest enough fellow, determin'd to let her be, or so he said. Yet tho' I determined I must watch him, I reflected there was but little I could do; he being the stronger, and I helpless in navigation without his skill.

I wonder'd she had tried to stay on the Cay, and said I believ'd it panick; but at this Venison laugh'd, saying mayhap she lusted after black skin; it being his opinion most planters' women do, but lack occasion for it. I was indignant at this libel, tho' half admitting it. 'Believe me,' cried he, 'had she remained there, there would have been no violation. For she would have lain freely to all three; and then, if ever she was rescu'd, had her dark lovers hang'd.'

We were rolling now into a turbulence, so I went below to seek out the subject of our parley. Diana, much tatter'd and hard-frowned, lay uneasy athwart a bunk. She eye'd me with no pleasure, and a great angry pouting; so seeking to make her easier, I told her how she would be put ashore, unharm'd, in France.

'Aye, and if I am, be sure my first act will be to have you clap't in jail,' said she.

'That were ungrateful of you,' I told her, 'for in preserving you from harm, Mr Venison and I are surely tempting our own providence.'

'You had better have left me on the Cay,' said she, 'as I desired.'

'To your destruction, girl!'

'Oh, la!' cried she. 'You do not know slave minds as I. They would never have dared harm me; and as for Nayle, he would see only guineas in my ransom.'

'Yet the slaves whipp'd you well,' I could not forbear to say.

'Yes!' cried she in a frenzy. 'And for each lash they will earn a thousand! As for you, boy, you too will writhe under it, for that is all that a slave understands.'

'I am no slave, except by accident and injustice.'

'Oh, but hearken! He who has been a slave remains one. Why! Were I a man, I would rather die than let them use me as they did you! But shackles were forged for you when you were born.'

At this I grew mightily vex'd, and drawing nearer to her, cried, 'And pride and cruel ignorance attended your birth at Meadowsweet.'

She rose up and lash'd her hand over my face. 'Never dare speak to me so!' cried she. And she stared in such a bitter passion that my own rage was overcome, and I stood trembling. 'Out of my sight!' she screamed, and snatch'd up a jug to hurl at me.

I battled with her, and she bit and spat and claw'd, then burst into a weeping. 'Oh!' cried she, her hair lank across her face. 'Is there no man worthy of me? My father, Horatio – all are weaklings!'

'I am a man,' said I.

'You!' cried she, tearing aside her locks. 'You – a brat!'

'Well,' said I to her, 'I am brat enough to be a father, or soon shall be.'

'Oh, la!' said she, and laugh'd. 'And who is the wife that is so fortunate?'

''Tis Priscilla,' said I, flushing up.

Her face turned all sour and twisted. 'Oh, you disgust me with your nastiness!' she cried. 'To father a brute! Is there no white man who can withstand it?'

'You were ready enough,' said I, 'to stay at the Cay with three such brutes.'

'Away from me!' she called out in a riot. 'Take your filth out of my presence, or I swear to slay you!'

I stood there irresolute in rage, for how dared she, my prisoner, a woman, a child younger than I, address me so! But what fire she had, and an authority! And though this should mean nothing now, I could not forget that to her, I had been a slave.

I told Venison of my displeasure with her, needing a confidant and consolation. But he laugh'd at me again, and said it was a child's quarrel, which pleased me no more. 'Lad,' said he, 'when once she is put ashore, you will be rid of her, and soon forget her. These planters' children are all corrupted, and not for an honest lad like you. But in the Americas, you will find girls who know modesty and diligence to serve a man.'

'But I had no thought,' said I 'of any life with such as Diana. 'Tis her ingratitude that so galls me, and her intemperate venom.'

We sailed on some days, the skies staying calm, and no sail sighted; Diana was in a pout: and vexed me by speaking with Venison as if they were two grown persons, and I a child. And for him she worked well, busy about the craft; and calling on me for menial tasks, as if I were a cabin boy.

I could see an anxiety in Venison, and enquired about it

when we were alone beside the wheel. It was that the
French island (called 'France') should have come up by now,
and he feared to be off course. There was also the food and
water, that we had loaded at St Laughter, growing slack. And
should we not sight the island soon, said Venison, we had best
tack and bear east. For there, he knew, was a chain of little
islands, all English, that we could hardly miss. And though
there was a great risk to me of putting in there, to die of
thirst and hunger were a greater. Besides, said he, we could
keep the girl lock'd, and I hid, while he went ashore alone to
seek for his bearings and get provender, which he could buy
with a few guineas remaining to him.

At this I said, why should we not, when we sailed off again
from this English island, put back there again by night, and
lay Diana ashore in a solitary spot upon the coast? For thus
she would come to no real harm, yet we would be rid of her;
and before she could raise any alarm about us, we would be
well away to France.

'Ha!' cried the colonist. 'You wish to unburden us of your
sweet enemy!'

'Nay, Mr Venison,' said I, 'but you must surely know that,
even in France, if we took her there, she could seek to harm
us by reporting on me to the French. For our nations are all
peaceful now, and once they are persuaded that she speaks
truly (I mean, being a rich planter's girl), they will believe
her to my cost.'

'Some truth in that, lad,' said the sailor. 'And I, too, want
for no troubles from the French lest my finding a ship to the
Americas be impeded.' So it was decided thus, and we tacked
east.

But Diana, who was no fool, noticed our changed course,

or at least our muttering, and asked us of it; to which Venison only told her fables till, forgetting her disdain of me, she began to pester; and when I said naught, to change her manner to me, and act prettily. 'Come, Alexander,' she said. 'There is some plan afoot, and I trust you mean no wickedness towards me.'

'No, I mean you well: far more than you merit for all your contumely.'

'Oh, la!' She reached out her two hands (for we were in the cabin) and held me round the elbow. 'Alexander,' she said earnestly, 'you should have some pity, and some understanding for me. Conceive to yourself the terrors and loneliness of a young girl, postured as I have been these fearful days! Ah!' she went on, coming closer and looking up, 'for you, these perils are as nothing, for you are a man. But I . . . Your life has been hard, Alexander, and perhaps fate has made me cause it to be more so. But please . . . oh, pray think of me a little!' And she fell against my chest and wept, looking up pitifully from time to time.

I knew of her wiles, yet knew I could not gainsay her. And truth, too, I had a little hope that she had some heart in her, and part of it for me. So sitting beside her, and holding her gently by me, I said she could take comfort, for we were putting her ashore on an English island, whence she could return safely to St Laughter.

But at this intelligence she stared at me, rose in a tempest, and cried that she wished to go to France (I mean the island) and no other place! I was astonished at this, for surely she would be further still, in distance and tribulation, from her home.

'But I hate St Laughter!' she cried out in a passion. 'That

horrid little rock I have always wanted to escape from! But France — France is a big island, with cities and fine people; and once I am there, I can force my foolish father to let me sail to Europe and my mother!'

'You fear not the French?' said I.

'Oh, but I have seen them, when their ships come to St Laughter, and their officers are angels, Alexander, very heroes. What grace and fire they have, beside our drunken ninnies!'

'But what of me, Diana? What will you tell the French when we get there, you who have sworn to have me jail'd and lash'd?'

At this she looked all penitence and submission, and throwing her arms about me, like a wanton child, she said, 'Ah, can you not trust me, Alexander? I know I am rash in my speech, and passionate, but can you believe that I would speak ill to harm you?'

'Why, yes,' said I, pulling away from her. 'I can believe it.'

Now love came into her warm eyes. 'Come,' she said, holding out her arms. 'See how I trust you, dear little white slave!'

It was a curious truth about Diana that tho' her deceits were so apparent, and she knew they must be, yet she practis'd them with such conviction that they could persuade not just herself, but even he who knew he was being trick'd. I have often wondered at this since; and believe her force consisted in that childishness she had, that seeming innocence not of heart, but of her years and education. For she believed utterly in the lie she told, tho' it was one in which even she herself, a moment before or after, did not believe at all!

'Kiss me, Alexander,' said she, and did not wait for my

reply. And she enfolded me as if I were the one love of her
life, the only being in the world! But when my blood rose and
I moved forwardly to her, she held me away, her eyes all reproach at me, and said, 'But Alexander, you would not take
vantage of my helplessness!' And so guileful was she, yet
moving with such assurance, that she possess'd the art to win a
man with her person without yielding it! For though I
struggled with her in a sudden heat, she turned to tears and a
remonstrance that quite dampened it.

In this affray, we were interrupted by a call from Venison;
and shaking with denied passion, I bestirr'd myself, and went
on deck. He pointed to sails that were approaching us, and
eyed them anxiously. For in these seas a small craft with so
few aboard, and little armed, and such a way from shore, sails
to its peril.

But we could be reassur'd; for they were fishermen from
France, the island, and hailing them, we learned we were far
nearer to it than Venison had supposed. At this we decided
that, come what may, we must change tack to France, and
did so; which much delighted Diana, to whom fate had
given her wish without any need of pleading to me further.

We came in sight of France at dusk, and saw this was no
small rock like St Laughter, but a territory that spread to the
horizons. Craft sped about us as we approach'd, plying busily;
and we could see that the port, lying before us (it was called
Avenir), was no village like clumsy Joie. But Venison
decided, against all Diana's protestations, that we would heave
to for the night, and sail up into Avenir next morning; for he
thought it prudent not to begin our probings and parleyings
in the dusk.

Now in sight of land, and hope revived (despite the dangers),

I could not but turn to Venison and say to him what was in my heart: which was that, since I had left Mortar, he was the first man who had behaved honestly to me, and not trick'd or harmed me. He laugh'd at this, though I think that he was pleased; and he told me I would make a good colonist in the Americas if I, too, dealt with them as frankly.

The French

A HIGHLANDER must have in his heart a warm place for the French, who, in our battles with the English, have been our friends; and had we triumphed with them, the shame of the Union would have been spared us. And yet, with my Lowland mother and the precepts of John Knox still informing my intelligence, I had also, I confess, a sort of suspicion of the French: of a licence and frivolity that, so I had been taught, sullied all their bravery and virtue.

It was thus in a divided spirit that I stepp'd ashore on this island, France; but this division did not long survive the wonders that I saw there. Avenir was the largest city (save for Bristol) that I had yet beheld; and not only so much vaster than little Joie, but infinitely more elegant and vivacious. In Joie, even the free trudg'd as if half slaves; in Avenir, even the slaves seemed light-footed. Of course, I knew well enough that they could not be happy; and true, I had learned by now that city slaves have a sort of deceitful liberty denied to those of the plantations — which, around Avenir, are enormous. But still, there was a sparkling, noisy eagerness about this place which, after our dismal days, delighted me.

Before we sailed in, Venison, putting on spectacles he had, drew up a paper: which said that Diana Newbury, of her own free will, and without any duress, acknowledged her fair treatment by us on the skiff; avowed that we had rescued her from the Cay; and swore in particular that Alexander Nairn was free from any guilt of her first removal from St Laughter. And this, said he, she must put her name to before we let her step ashore.

'But Mr Venison,' said I, 'she can deny all this and say 'twas forced. Besides, it is hardly true I did not plot with the slaves to take her off the island.'

'Well, this paper may make it hard for her to speak,' said he. 'And if we make haste to sell the boat, and get away, she cannot harm you much.'

'Could we not keep her prisoner on the boat till you have sold it?'

'Boy, you know her well,' he said, 'and to hold her in the harbour will be to cage a vixen. Believe me, she will try any device to 'scape, but if we let her go freely, she is less apt to annoy us.'

When he put the paper before Diana, she read it gravely and said she would set her name to it; and added in her own hand, and freely, that she owed her life to us, and would forever be our debtors. Then smiling and handing this to us like a queen to her servitors, she began making ready, as best she could, to primp her young beauty for the bedazzlement of the inhabitants of France. And so we sailed in with a light wind, and hopefully.

On the quay she bade us farewell with all the dignity of French Queen Marie. And when we asked her did she not wish an escort till she could find the Governor (or whoever she intended to enlist to help her), she thanked us prettily, and said nay. 'Farewell, pretty young slave,' she murmur'd to me, 'may the heavens protect you, as we all have need.' And with this she set off up the mole, as if she were princess of Avenir, and I felt the loss of her more than I had imagin'd; and also, with all her wickedness, a kind of jealous admiration of her spirit.

Then Venison set out on shore, to see about our business, leaving me to guard the boat, and promising no delay; for he could see all my anxiety to explore in Avenir. While I waited there, some French lads approach'd me, sailors of their navy, and asked me who I was, and whence. When they heard how ill my French was, they frown'd on me, believing me to be an Englishman; but they grew fairer when I said Scottish, and said I must come and toast Prince Charles with them, who was now safe in their country. So eager was I to see in the harbour, that I asked an honest old salt (with but one leg) to keep observance on our boat a while, and I set off with these matelots into the hurlyburly of the city; which I must say seemed to me as boisterous as a carnival. They carried me to rum-shops where we drank more punches than I can remember, till I woke up in the arms of a mulatto woman, in a place I knew not, with a head like the explosion of a hundred cannon.

When at length I came back onto the quay, much asham'd and truly woebegone, I found our boat was vanish'd; and while standing in a perplexity, was boarded by the old salt of yesterday, who handed me this letter:

'Alexander,
    'Think not ill of me, lad, but a boat is putting out tonight for Cuba, which is in a fair direction for me; but they cannot take me as crew, needing none, so I must needs be passenger, and pay. Of this the cost is much the same as the little I could get for our old boat, in a swift sale. So I have paid my passage, and am away.

149

'Had you been here, perchance could I have persuaded them to take you for a child's fee; but you were gone, and I could attempt nothing. I have ten guineas over from the sale (after paying of the passage), of which I have given five to the old sailor; with the promise of one to him from you if, as I hope, he prove honest. I could do no more, not knowing where you were.

'Farewell, young shipmate. I hope to see you one fairer day in Delaware.

'Absolem Venison.'

At this I was much cast down and burst, to my shame, into a weeping. The old salt sought to console me, and handed me a single guinea which, he swore, was all that Venison had left for me. I was too dejected for any argument and, first gazing sadly out to sea, turned back into the port; thinking if rum had betrayed me yesterday, perhaps it would be my friend today.

In a city unknown to him, and where he has once drunken, the footsteps of the stranger carry him back thither; and I soon found myself returned to the bordello. 'Ah, *mon petit*, you come back to greet your beauty?' said the female in the saloon, with affability. I said sadly no, and begged but for a rum; fearing a little of my reception, I avow, for I was not sure if my sailor friends had discharg'd all the debts of yesterday. But I need not have been uneasy; for when she brought me the punch, the French lady was all smiles, and had poured herself another at my default, not needing to ask, said she, being positive of my open-handed nature.

She was Mlle Doute, she said, the morning woman of the place when few were attending (this she said with a sigh), and

as I could see ... *si charmant* though I was, I must perceive it
... past her first flush of youth. (Indeed, she was a stringy,
painted bawd of some forty winters). Yes, she continued, *Sans
Regrets* (this was the name of the stew) was languid at this
hour. And this was true; for all its luxury hung heavy, with a
stench of rum and sweat. But, she continued, from the afternoon onward, when the girls rose and the gallants flock'd, it
was quite otherwise – a frolic. So I could wait, perhaps, till
then; though if my desire press'd, or my ship was sailing, she
could call a sleeping strumpet to bestir herself.

To this I rejoined that alas, I could no longer command the
gallantry of last night, since I was now quite bereft. She
stared hard on me at this, but begged me to continue: and so,
looking as young and gentle as I might, I unfolded my sad
story to her, or parts of it.

On hearing of it, she humm'd and cluck'd, for if no one
likes to hear a stranger possesses nothing, in a brothel they
like to hear it even less. But she seemed not unfriendly, and
said perhaps something could be done; but that first she must
speak with Mme Plénitude, who was the Empress of this
paradise. But this lady would be slumbering now, and could
not yet be disturb'd. Of course (she said smiling) she could
depend upon it, I was a grateful lad; and that could she secure
employment for me (and here she darted a meaning simper at
me), she knew I would be eager to show my thanks by
Favours to her.

At this there entered on the room, from the recess within,
a huge mulatto, a very giant, rubbing his great eyes with
monster fists. Him she presented as Hercule, the porter of the
place, or peace-keeper; and he consented to join us in a glass
from what remained of my poor guinea. She told him of my

predicament, but he doubted what I could do for service, since Mme Plenitude had slaves for all the labour. But perhaps something could be arranged; and at that he gave me a smile all fill'd with teeth, and a Look so marked (brac'd with a meaning caress beneath the table), that I saw my virtue would be sore besieged, were I to be employed at *Sans Regrets*. And yet I hoped that I might be accepted there. For what better place to hide in while I waited to find a ship to carry me away?

At length Mlle Doute, who had pluck'd up her skirts and gone to parley, return'd to say that Mme Plénitude would grant me audience; and I was ushered up to the broad balcony that lined the inner courtyard of the stew. Here Doute knock'd on a wide door and, when bidden, push'd me in.

Mme Plénitude lay in a huge bed, much rumpl'd, as if just vacated by a regiment. She was a large woman, lavishly adorn'd, and two slaves were busy with her hair and toilet; while from an adjacent shelf, another served her a collation. She eyed me in silence for a while then said, in a deep tho' silvery accent, 'Well, boy?'

I said that I wished to be of service to her; and that I was an honest lad, and willing.

'Honest!' cried she. 'Tell me: could you say the whole truth about yourself, and still tell me you are honest?'

'I mean, Madam,' I replied, 'that whatever the world may say, my heart is honest.'

'Not quite the same,' she said, biting a peel'd mango. 'And in this House, boy, what the world says, matters much. However: tell me this. Have you any hatred towards France?'

'Madam, I swear not,' said I.

'*Brave garçon*,' she said, nodding her wigg'd head. 'Well,

perhaps I can make use of you. To my establishment there come mostly, thank God, Frenchmen. But Avenir is a great port – the finest in the Antilles. And hither, there voyage seamen of all races including, alas, English.'

I bowed in apology for this.

'Who,' she proceeded, 'besides being drunken and quarrelsome, are to me personally, rebarbative. However: I am a woman of business; and since they pay well – I see to that, I can assure you – I receive, if I do not welcome them.'

'That shows your generous spirit, Madame.'

'*Tais-toi*. Now, most of these barbarians speak no French; and it would be of use to me to have a reliable lad here who could work in my saloon to interpret their wishes and, more to the point, reconcile them to mine.'

'I am your man, Madame,' said I.

'That we shall see. I can promise you, of course, no wages, only board, though gratuities you may hope for. As for your physical needs, I would ask you to remember at all times that the girls – I mean my Ladies, I do not speak to you of the slaves – are reserved exclusively for paying visitors. Should you make money, you may approach them, through me, like any other; but not otherwise; and if you attempt it, I shall see that you make the acquaintance of my old friend, the Captain of the Guard, who has as many dungeons as I have bedrooms. Is that clear?'

'Perfectly, Madame.'

'Be off with you, then. Ask Hercule, on my part, to attire you in a style more appropriate to *Sans Regrets*. Adieu!'

The Rising

A N D S O I became a pander of her house, tho' spending each instant I could snatch close on the quay, or in the seamen's taverns, trying to find ships. Part of my trouble was my youth and inexperience, for there were many well-season'd men adrift in Avenir, seeking berths. Another part was that perhaps I was less eager to leave the island than I fancied.

At *Sans Regrets*, though I first met with some hostility, I was soon accepted, chiefly because of my unfailing deference (not quite unfeign'd) to Mme Plénitude; who, though haughty to me, was gracious too, praising my diligence in the saloon. With the French clients I soon became a favourite – *le petit Ecossais* they called me, and gave me gold; while with the English, I was a very diplomat. Hercule was jealous of me, till I let him win money from me at cards, which pleased his avarice; and to Mlle Doute I was so attentive and respectful, offering her flowers and keepsakes, that I half persuaded her I thought her a being too august for one so lowly to expect any favours from. With the Ladies of the house, I preserved a prudent attitude of decorum – one *correcte,* as Mme Plénitude declared with approbation.

The hours were long, interminable indeed, as in all places of debauchery, whose chief purpose is less to give vein to licence, than to murder time. I also must drink much, ruining my digestion, for to refuse a toast from a guest annoyed Mme Plénitude exceedingly. There was a great tedium, too (that I had scarce suspected), in contemplating vice, not as one who enjoys it, but as a pimp who helps in its supply.

One evening, some officers had come and, as often happened (much to the vexation of the Ladies, and the more so of their Abbess), they chatter'd among themselves, drinking the hours, and bestowing on the neglected girls no more than a lazy pinch, or blow upon a passing rump.

'Oh, the little prude is a wanton, depend upon it,' cried the one.

'An English *saint ni touche* if e'er I saw one!'

'And sure she was roll'd on the sand when the slaves took hold of her.'

'And by the pirates who brought her here, I warrant. Have they been taken?'

'No – fled. She surely bribed them to make off, so they could tell no tales.'

'And now, by your leave, she is the toast of Avenir, even ogled by His Excellency.'

'The pet of the Governor's lady, too, which is more remarkable.'

'Oh, Her Excellency is devout, and a great protector of innocence.'

'Torrent, I hear, has quite lost his heart to her.'

'But not his prick: her English legs stay well knit.'

'Ah, but she shall open them to any planter, if she finds one rich enough.'

'And whose priest knows the wedding service . . .'

'Poor Torrent, with only his lieutenant's pay! What hope has he?'

I knew who they were speaking of, and tho' I would cry silence on them, longed to hear more, if but to hear her name.

But as it is often to the spy, they changed their theme.

'Yet another revolt suppress'd. You heard?'

'Aye, at Mazarin.'

'Twelve slaves hang'd, the whole plantation whipp'd.'

''Tis the republicans at home who stir them.'

'Impossible: they cannot read or write, so what can they hear?'

'Revolt travels on the winds.'

'Over the Atlantic?'

'There have been countless small risings on the island. One day, they will not be small.'

'In metropolitan France as well, I doubt not.'

''Tis the fault of the English, who first slew a king, and so undermined authority.'

'Give me a company, and guns, and whips, and I shall defy any slaves or rabble.'

'Master regicide! Bring us more brandy!'

This was intended for my ears and, feigning docility, I brought them spirits. Mme Plénitude, meanwhile, rising from her throne on a dais in the saloon, where she had been engaged in converse with some plump planters, approached the officers as if a general come to rebuke their sloth, and summon them to duty.

'Fie, gentlemen!' cried she, pinching a cheek here, tousling a head there. 'What will they think of you, the handsomest women of Avenir, if you leave them to languish in their boudoir?'

'Ah, but tonight, Madame,' said one, 'we must conserve our energies and gravity for His Excellency's reception. Tomorrow is King Louis' birthday, you must remember.'

'Could I forget the blessed anniversary of our Monarch?

But this glorious event, gentlemen, should not prevent your celebration in a more vigorous manner.'

'Ah, dear Madame, we shall surely return here when our formal duties have been properly performed.'

'So I should hope. Meanwhile, be off with you, and no more brandy; for the sooner you kiss Her Excellency's arse the faster you may return to embrace those of my young Ladies.'

Thus admonish'd, the officers rose, clinking swords, to do their duty, followed soon by the rich planters, also bidden to the petty palace of Avenir. So that inside *Sans Regrets*, there was an unusual emptiness, and tranquility, the girls playing cards and bickering with boredom, and Mme Plénitude, rebuking them shrill-voic'd from time to time, ensconced with a single visitor, a plain stocky man of middle age in spectacles, who drank little, but listened attentively and respectfully to all his hostess said.

Having but little work to do, and the heat torrid, I saunter'd in the courtyard under the stars. Around the yard, and on the balconies, the slaves were busy with their tasks; or rather, seeming busy, in that style of domestic serfs, especially in a brothel, whose whole end is dedicated to sloth. Yet to me, even remembering the heat, and the celebrations outside in the city, the slaves seemed, that evening, unusually turgid; and, what was not customary, forward and malapert in their behaviour. They threw bold defiant looks that made me wonder.

There is, in the attitude of masters towards their slaves, one paradox among many; which is that, tho' the masters pretend the slaves are of no consequence, with all thoughts other than survival beaten from their brains, the masters are ever anxious about what passes in those sullen minds. Another contradiction I had noticed is that whereas the masters, having power, believe themselves all-knowing, the slaves, who have none, can in reality examine their masters very nearly, and grow to know them well; far better, indeed, than the masters do them, to whom the slaves are only names. Yet while the masters like to believe the slaves know nothing of them, except what they permit them to understand, they remain uneasy lest the slaves might know far more than they should. Which, indeed, they do; for the victim, to exist, must study his oppressor far more closely than the oppressor must study him.

When I returned to the saloon, the gentleman with spectacles was alone, and called me over. He bade me be seated, offered me a glass, and asked me was I English? Well, Scottish, sir, said I, and he, was he not English too? Aye, said he, a ship's captain on a visit here, with his boat lying on the further shore. And were there, he asked, many English in Avenir at present?

I told him what I could, which was that no English vessels were in port, but that Avenir being the chief city of the Caribbean, it had many English traders settled there. Did I know where they all lived, asked he? Well some, indeed most, I knew of, since they huddl'd in a nearby district close together. And English women, he said? The merchants' wives, I answered, and their daughters. And fresh arrivals, he enquir'd?

I had not purposed to speak to him of Diana, out of a sort of precaution, but so strong was my instinct to pronounce her name, that I did so. 'Aye,' said he. 'Diana Newbury from St Laughter, is she not? I have heard some gossip of her.'

I said nothing to this, and became aware that this Captain was staring at me sharply, tho' with eyes blink'd by his spectacles; and with his hands on both his knees, like claws, he sat quite still waiting for me to say something more. And the feeling grew on me as he stay'd silent, that all his questions were not to dispel his ignorance, but to discover what I knew, or how much I would say.

Then, after a long pause, 'And you, lad, how did you chance to Avenir?'

'I came to St Laughter,' I replied, 'upon a slaver. And hearing this island was a richer place, I shipp'd here to seek employment.'

'Shipp'd here how?'

'Why, upon a boat.'

'I did not suppose you swam. Which boat?'

'Sir,' I said, rising, 'I thank you for the spirits, but you are curious.'

His hand quick grasp'd my wrist. 'Indeed I am, boy,' said he. 'Tell me which boat!'

Hercule looked over at his raised voice and I tried to signal the mulatto; but just at this moment I was spared further traffic with the Captain because a French officer enter'd, who I saw to be Monsieur Torrent. He came staggering near our table and, greeting me, cried, 'Scot, bring me a bottle!' So I wrench'd my hand hard from the Captain's, and went to serve him.

'Boy,' said he, 'you are too young to know it, but all life is a snare.'

'Aye, sir,' said I.

''Tis crapulous!' he cried. 'For what can life offer to a man? Two satisfactions only: his work, his woman! Now, as to work, here am I exiled in a colony, far from glory and promotion. And as to woman, I am bewitch'd by a Huguenot bitch.'

'There are other ladies to chose from, sir,' said I.

'Ah, but not when the spell is cast by a witch fit for your

countryman, Macbeth! Or if not a witch, a ravening huntress. Well is she named Diana!'

'You have just left her, sir?'

'Aye, boy, where, at the Governor's ball, from under the folds of Her Excellency's skirts, she teases the trousers of each officer of the garrison!'

'Go then, sir, and be teas'd!'

'To what purpose, lad? All I can offer is my beauty and my valour; but she dances with stout colonels and the aristocracy of sugar.'

I had noticed the strange Captain, with a hard glance at us, departing; and on an impulse, I cried to the lieutenant, 'But you who are a Frenchman, sir; of whom the chief attribute is audacity! Return to Government House! Assail her! Board her! Hoist your ensign on the proud pinacles of her mainmast!'

He stood, then totter'd back. 'Come, lieutenant, I shall be your pilot,' I said, hoisting him to his feet.

Out in the streets of Avenir, the stir was up in the warm air. Of course, this was a night of festival; but the animation had a shrill sharpness, an uneasy swell. There were unaccustomed buffets, sudden surges, shouts, rushes, leapings, then pools of silence. There came songs like cries, drums deafening, laughter into a yell.

The *château* blaz'd: inside the brilliance, outside the sweated dark; for round about the centre that held the ball, the slaves turned, crying with ecstasy and hate. The Lieutenant and I pushed through, sometimes spun in a spiral, or obliquely; so that when we reached the great outer staircase, we were thrown up it falling backward.

I stood with the servants in the entrance hall, peering in at a disorder that seemed one moment celebration, the next riot:

for windows crack'd, lights split, there were swarms, oaths and yells. Of the slaves, pack'd hot, most seemed bewilder'd, some huddled by their masters, others drew knives, seized weapons, shot, hack'd. Men ran in confusion, fear, or deadly purpose, and blood spill'd. Outside, the crowd raised a bellow and, with a great gasp, clatter'd roaring up the steps into the hall.

I ran into the ballroom, jostling hot beating bodies, lights cracking flames, calling widly for Diana. But my cry was lost in cries. Strangers, with rough purpose in the din and tumult, ran in, tracked down bodies, seized and dragged them through smashed windows. A blow stunn'd me, I was dropt like a sack onto the lemon lawn, pick'd up, and pulled into a carriage, pack'd with others, which jerk'd, lurched and raced off trampling the crowd. The masked men held pistols, and commanded silence.

Outside the town, in felt darkness and with the only sound our horses and whistling wheels, I could see, at bends in the still country, that we were several coaches fleeing out of Avenir. We raced on for miles, with stray shots fired out of the sugar cane, and pistol cracks back at the darkness from our guards. On the mountains, there were fires, gleaming like vol-canoes, and a rush of wind. After hours we tumbled into a bay, were haul'd out, steered down the shingle, and put into boats that rowed out to a huge hulk in the moonlight. The oarsmen were bent and silent, the captives huddl'd up and moaning.

'Where are we going?' I asked a rower.

'On *Scorpion*.'

'And what is that?'

'Yonder ship.'

'Whose is it?'

'The ship of your saviour, Captain Nayle.'

The Captain

LIKE all boys, I had read tales of pirates, and had supposed
something of hot colour, and a sort of evil romance: a hell-
ship wickedly superb, with a wild luxury of demons like an
Arabian dream. But such the *Scorpion* was not: it was an
ordinary boat, much like our slaver; and for the crew, except
that they seemed of mixed parentage, with many blacks, there
was naught to distinguish them from those of a more usual kind.

This I observ'd when dawn found us out to sea, and heading south; and I beheld, lying around me on the deck, some
twenty or more persons of both sexes, mostly of the substantial
kind, dress'd for festivity, though now soiled and torn; and all,
when they spoke (for they seemed to know one another), appearing to be English. I tried to make converse with them, but
they eyed me askance, as if not one of them; so I determined
to spy upon their parley, hoping to learn more of what all this
might portend.

'Aye,' said one. 'Nayle again. Another ransom.'

'True, but he saved us from the fury of the slaves.'

'He must have had wind of their revolt, and come to make
us buy our lives.'

'Wind of it! For aught we know, 'twas Nayle who stirr'd
up the slaves!'

'The French cannot control them: they are too frivolous
and lax.'

'Believe me, Nayle has a triple purpose: to annoy the

French, to save us for ransom, and to show our government
he is one of the worthy pirates: those that assault only foreign
ships, protecting Britons.'

'That shall not save him from hanging in his time.'

'When they catch him . . . Where will he carry us?'

'To St Laughter, I doubt not. Then the cost of a ransom,
and a ship back again to France.'

'And repair to our homes and warehouses, for they are surely
burn'd down and looted, if not by the slaves, the French.'

'A curse on them all. The French are not worthy to own
slaves.'

'We should seize their islands, as we have done to some
already.'

'Are we all here on deck? There are merchants of Avenir I
do not see, who are doubtless slain, or hiding.'

'Well, I saw some stowed below last night, as well.'

'The richer, you may be bound, all given cabins. He has a
fortune with this cargo, for all will pay his price.'

''Twill earn him a knighthood from His Majesty.'

'Or to be made Governor to boot.'

'Nay, nay – Nayle will hang on the yardarm soon, I
promise you.'

'Hush: here comes his Mate.'

But it was I whom the Mate beckoned, and he carried me
to the Captain's cabin; where, as I had half feared, I met
again the spectacled stranger who had quizzed me at *Sans
Regrets*. He greeted me coolly, and said I might be seated.
And then,

'Now boy, you are to tell me the whole truth of how you
came to Avenir. Before you begin, remember this: I know
more than you may think I do; and on this ship, we have a

way with liars. It is a cruel way, and it does not fail us.' He looked at me in a calm and patient style, his hands clasped, seeming strangely like a Minister, in his sober mien.

'Sir,' said I, 'I sailed to Avenir with a seaman from America, a colonist called Venison.'

'Aye, and who else?'

'An English lady, sir, from St Laughter, called Miss Newbury.'

'So,' said he. 'Now this American: where has he gone to?'

'To Cuba, so he said.'

'He told you this?'

'No, sir. He left a message for me telling it.'

'I see. Now, whence did you sail into Avenir?'

'From a Cay, sir, whose name I know not.'

'And how came you to this Cay?'

'From St Laughter, sir.'

'Aye, but how?'

'In a boat owned by one Marrowbone: he, and I, and the lady.'

'None other?'

'No, sir.'

'On the same boat as brought you into Avenir?'

'Aye, sir.'

'And why came you to the Cay?'

'In truth, sir, to offer our services, and the lady for ransom, both to you.'

'That were kindly of you, boy. Yet I remained perplex'd. For you sail out of St Laughter with a seaman Marrowbone, and sail into Avenir with a seaman Venison.'

''Tis true, sir. Venison and I met upon the Cay, and so he came with me to Avenir.'

'And what befell Marrowbone?'

'He tumbled in the sea, sir.'

'Tumbled in?'

'Aye, sir.'

'And when he had so tumbled, you sailed the boat alone into the Cay?'

'I am a seaman, sir.'

'Aye, I warrant you are.'

He took some snuff, not looking down, still gazing at me steady. 'And this Venison,' said he. 'Did he speak to you of any secret on the Cay?'

'Aye, sir, a treasure. A treasure that belonged to you.'

''Tis true it belonged to me. He brought it onto your boat from out the Cay?'

'Nay, sir, he brought nothing but himself.'

There was a silence, then he said, 'Boy, my Mate must take you down below.'

'Sir, it is as I say. He did not say to me that he had found your treasure. And even had he found it, there was no time to put anything aboard. We were but a short while on the Cay, and then we fled.'

'Fled?'

'Left the Cay, sir. He hated it, and was most eager to depart.'

'What did he fear?'

'Perchance that you might suddenly return there, sir.'

'Aye, perchance.'

'Sir! If he had taken any treasure from the Cay, I must have known of it. And if I knew it would I have stepped off our boat in Avenir till I had part of it?'

'He could have tricked you . . .'

'No, he sailed off to Cuba, as I told you, with only the value of our boat.'

'To Cuba. You are sure he sailed there?'

'Aye, sir. I asked in the port, at Avenir, and the ship for Cuba had indeed sailed, and he on it.'

'So he could not have sailed back to the Cay to lift the treasure.'

'Impossible. Beside he was on the ship for Cuba, I saw our own boat he had barter'd, lying in the dock at Avenir.'

'And boy: you have told none other of this treasure?'

'None, sir, I swear!'

He waited, then said quietly, 'Then we are left with a mystery, boy.'

'Sir?'

'I returned to the Cay after your visit there. And the treasure – it was gone.'

'Gone, sir!'

'Aye, gone. And the question that irks me is, who took it?'

This he asked me not in a fierce or hectoring tone, but in a reasonable way, as if 'twere some puzzle, perhaps in mathematicks, wherein I could help him to a solution. Yet I was not deceiv'd, and knew him deadly.

'Sir,' said I, 'I know not. But sure, this Cay can be no secret place, and others in these seas beside yourself must know of it. They could have gone there and found your treasure.'

'To know the Cay,' said he, 'is not to know where the treasure was hid.'

'I can help you no further, sir.'

'No, boy? But what if others can?'

'Sir?'

166

'On the Cay, you tell me, there were three: you, who knew nothing; Venison who sails to Cuba; and who else?'

'Why, Miss Diana, sir, who is in Avenir, and I trust protected.'

He smiled at me. 'No, boy,' said he. 'She is on this ship.'

At this I fell into such blushing and confusion, yet an anger too that he should play with me like a cruel cat. At length I said, 'And she has told you?'

He shook his head slowly. 'No, boy,' he said, 'she has refused.' He smiled again. 'She refuses a pirate on a pirate ship,' and now he laughed, though sadly. 'But boy,' he said earnestly, 'her I cannot torture. For consider: would a father pay a ransom for a shrivell'd daughter? Nay. But you, boy . . . Well, I had better send you to the Mate. You will be back here in half an hour to tell me everything. He will see you are not too distress'd to speak . . .'

'Captain Nayle,' I said. 'May I speak with her before you do this?'

He looked at me, musing; then called the Mate, and told him to carry me to Miss Newbury's cabin, and not let me out of view. The merchants on the deck, who seemed refreshed now, glanced as if they guessed at some disgrace, and wanted no knowledge of anyone who might impede their safe delivery on shore.

At the sight of me, she showed neither pleasure, loathing, nor surprise. Gazing haughtily at the Mate, she bade him wait outside her cabin, and would not speak further till he withdrew. And then she cried out, 'Oh, that ninny Nayle who has spoil'd everything! Her Excellency had promised me the next boat to Bordeaux!'

'But the rising, the peril to you from the slaves!'

'Peril! Slaves! They can stab in the night treacherously, but without will or courage how can they rebel? They will be hanging in hundreds at Avenir today!'

'No, they will not be defeated yet: the rising was too big, too bloody.'

'You do not know slaves! They are born to defeat! You may tremble if you wish, but I know them too well for fear.'

She had always this art to vex me, so I said, 'Well, if slaves do not trouble you, you should at least fear Nayle.'

She looked at me with disdain. 'Not one of us of consequence on the islands fears any Nayle. For a nothing like you, a pirate is a fearsome being. But we know them well! They are licensed thieves, and 'tis they who fear our anger. For never forget! Our Navy sails to protect our trade. If Nayle and his kind do not trouble *that*, they are allowed their jackal calling. But let any English pirate lay hands upon a planter . . .'

I must, despite myself, admire her effrontery, and thought (as before) how in this world, to believe you are born powerful is half to be so. Then, asking her patience, I told her of the cruel threat to me from Nayle; but she soon interrupted me. 'Oh, I know all about that treasure on the Cay!' she cried.

'How can you?'

'Because the American told you of it, while I lay bound upon the beach, your voices rose, and I have ears.'

'Then who took it?'

'The slaves, of course.'

'But how could they know of it?'

She smiled as if at a fool. 'While we struggled on the shore, I cried out to Daniel, "The treasure! Seek the treasure!"'

'Why did you tell him this?'

She shrugged.

'And if he heard you, how could he find it?'

'I can guess. The slave Bandele is an African. We know on the plantations what a nose and eye they have for traces we cannot see of any secret place a man, or animal, has been to . . .'

'But why did you tell them of it? And why, Diana, did you yearn to stay on the Cay with them, when we sought to rescue you?'

'Rescue me! You wanted me on the boat, alone, to do me violence, and make money from me.'

'We did you no violence!'

'Oh, but you tried, have you forgotten? But did Daniel try? A slave, yet he saw I was not harmed!'

'If he protected you, it was to deliver you up safe to Nayle.'

'Was it so? Who says it was? What I tell you, and know, is this. Between slaves that I can master, and a confess'd pirate like Venison with a ragamuffin boy, if I seek protection, I choose the slaves!'

'That is not why you sought to choose them on the Cay.'

'Why then?'

'Because you lusted after them!'

'Fool, fool, fool!' she cried in a great passion. 'What do you know of me, or slaves, or anything! It was you who dragg'd me on the boat for lust!'

I held her, and cried, 'No, for love, Diana!'

'Love!' she exclaimed in a hysterick shout. 'You! Love! No, 'twas jealousy – you are base enough to be jealous of a slave!'

These yellings brought in the Mate, whom I prevailed upon with difficulty to give us a short moment more. We were both silent a while, she breathing hard, and I said, 'Say what you will: but it is because of some feeling for Daniel that you would not tell Nayle about the slaves' presence on the Cay.'

She eyed me with malice. 'And why,' she asked, 'would you not tell him of it? For what had you to fear, if you had done so?'

'In truth,' I said, 'in truth . . .' but what was the truth about my silence?

'Well, "in truth" . . .'

At last I said, 'I wished the slaves no ill, for they had not harmed me, indeed helped. And had I told Nayle that they were on the Cay, I feared he would seek them out to kill them, once he discovered it was not Venison or I who took the treasure.'

She shook her head. 'That is not the real reason for your silence. The real reason, 'tis that *you* are a slave, and love them that they are!'

I said nothing to this, then asked her, 'How did they make away from the Cay without a boat?'

'I know not, except for this. There are a thousand Cays in the Caribbean. On some there are men with small craft that voyage to and fro . . . Even canoes of the Caribes sail great distances, for we have often seen them off St Laughter. So if the slaves were taken off, they could be anywhere . . .'

'And what would they do with a treasure on some other barren Cay?'

'Who knows? But one thing is certain. If they still have it, they have power, for men with gold do not have to linger on a Cay. And perchance, having power, they have some plan to use it.'

The Mate opened up the door and beckoned. 'So what must I do?' I asked. 'Tell Nayle?'

She laughed. 'What care I? Betray Daniel and his friend, or let Nayle wring it all from you, as you wish.'

And indeed, thought I, what loss could there be now in telling Nayle of Daniel and Bandele? For I consoled myself by thinking that if they had got far away, and with the treasure, even Nayle with his craft and knowledge of the islands would never find them. So when I was brought before him, I avowed that while I had told no lie, I had not told all the truth; and so reveal'd it to him.

Nayle listened to me carefully, flying into no rage at all, and seeming to be a man (I thought of a Minister again) to whom the pure truth, of itself, was of more import than any profit. Then after a pause, and pondering, he said,

'Boy, you have lied to me once, and you must not do so again. One further lie . . .' – he rais'd a finger, and then snapp'd it down, like a head cut. 'I tell you this,' he continued, 'because you must stay with me henceforward. For I shall find this pair, if I have to comb each isle of the West Indies!' He looked hard at me. 'But without you, boy, I shall not know their evil faces. But when we meet them . . . why! You will tell me who they are!'

'But, sir,' I said, 'the Caribbean seas are vast!'

'And I, boy, have sailed all my life in them, and shall never leave them till . . .' he smiled.

Encouraged by this smile, I said, 'Captain Nayle – 'tis but one treasure! How can it mean so much to a man like you? I mean, sir, are there not richer to be had which, if you pursue this pair, may fall to others?'

The Captain looked melancholy at this, and said to me

gravely, 'Lad, piracy, a century ago, was a brilliant occupation in these waters. Indeed, even the King's ships were privateers, and who was government ship, who pirates, one could scarcely tell! But alas! The governments are more powerful now – our own, French, Spanish, Portugese or Dutch – the trade is all in sugar and not gold, the navies assault each other only in a war. So that piracy is much declin'd, to petty plunders, ransoms – even trading! Aye, boy . . . ' and he smiled wanly ' . . . there are pirates who have sunk to trade!

'But in every pirate's life, as in each man's,' he continued, looking more cheerful and pecking at his snuff, 'there comes a great moment, as it did to me when I seized on this treasure that I have for a moment lost! Aye!' cried he, growing for the first time excited. ' 'Twas a Danish ship; and as you may know, the Danes are rare, though present, in these waters, and hence unprotected by any fleet. This boat came bringing muskets for the Dons in Panama, where there had been some revolt of the Caribes; and some suppression of it that the Spaniards, or their Jesuits, did not approve of, so that arms had to be smuggled in. I watched this boat sailing east with scant attention, believing it would sell its guns for sugar. But word reach'd me (for I have many spies, as all skill'd pirates must) that the Danes, greedy, perhaps, or being themselves some sort of pirate, asked gold for their guns, not goods, as used to be the custom before trade bedevill'd our craft in the Caribbean.

'This gold, boy, I took from them: the first, in truth, I had seen in such proportions, for little gold sails now and, when it does, in convoys that are unassailable. That gold I carried into the Cay, to wait a fit time for its fair disposal.

'So now, lad, do you understand my eagerness? For consider!

It is not only this wealth, for far more is at stake! My crew, the most honest pirates of these seas, know that we took it; and wonder why they have not got their share. Each pirate of the Caribbean knows of my triumph; and wonders I still sail in this old boat which, truth to tell, though I love it dearly, is leaky as a sieve, and rotted! So you can see, boy, the import of these two slaves to me; and what joy I had to discover you, lad, who will help me to recover what they robbed me of.'

I listened astounded to this narration, and could scarcely forbear to say to him, 'But Captain, do you not fear I may betray you?'

At this he gave me a glance that made me shudder, and said in a soft voice, 'No, boy, for you are henceforth as precious to me as my only son.'

Whereat his cabin door burst open, with the Mate crying, 'Captain, a sail! 'Tis a Portugoose!'

'A Portugoose?' cried Nayle, snatching up a telescope and rushing out.

Upon the deck, the crew were all scurrying, making ready for their assault, and the captive merchants lining the rail eagerly, as if spectators at a play. 'Twas some time before, casting my eye about the waters, I could discern the object of the pirate's fury, which was a craft of perhaps ten tons, a sloop, that wallowed in the easy seas a half mile off.

I brac'd myself for the thunder and tumult which, I believed, a pirate boarding would display, but here I was wrong, for thus was not Nayle's tactic. Instead, in silence save for the flapping of sheer'd sails, and the smack of the *Scorpion* turning on the waves, the Captain, moving his ship inward, began circling the sloop like a terrier around a mouse. As we drew closer to it, and could discern the posture of the Portuguese (who seemed about a dozen), I was surprised to see them kneeling as if in prayer and, save for their cries to providence, not otherwise preparing to resist. At length, a great gesture of the *Scorpion*'s might was made: from the bow, a ball was released from an old cannon, flying high up over the sloop, and with a bellow so deafening that all leapt in dismay; the more so as the cannon, backfiring as was not intended (or so I must suppose), shatter'd the carved woodwork of the rails, and laid Nayle's bombardier flat and groaning on the deck. The merchants, on recovery from their shock, let out a loud huzzah at this terror which an English pirate (tho' he was also robbing them) could strike into foreign hearts.

We now came alongside the sloop, and a boarding party, led by the Mate, clamber'd onto its deck, flourishing cutlasses in a fearful manner. Some disappeared below, and came up, helped by the captive crew, lugging casks and bales much split and tatter'd, which seemed to be all the treasure of the ship. The Portuguese officers were brought on board, and greeted civilly by Nayle; and from among the sloop's crew, lined up beneath him on the deck, he picked out a few lustier fellows to be press-gang'd. The remainder, letting out a pitiful wail, were made to walk no plank, nor even cutlass'd, but pluck'd up bodily by Nayle's men, and hurled into the sea. When all else were safe below, we sheer'd off, circled, and then sailing in majestically once more, ramm'd the gutted sloop to doom. His naval task completed, Captain Nayle, with much ceremony, presented the captured flag of the Portuguese to the senior among the merchants.

We sailed on after this engagement without any event, save that a restlessness became apparent among the merchants, with cries and grumbles as if they were plotting at some mutiny. By this time they had grown to accept me (the more so, as they now fancied me to be a favourite of Nayle), and I learned from a rope chandler the cause of their displeasure.

This was, that Nayle had broken his promise to carry them to St Laughter, and was making course northward to the chief city of this group of English islands, called Resurrection. 'Which means,' quoth the chandler, 'he will ask us all double ransom.'

'How so, sir?' I enquir'd.

'Because the rogue knows full well that our agents in Resurrection hold ten times the wealth of those trading in St Laughter.'

'Then why did he not sail there in the first place?'

'Because St Laughter, having no Governor, cannot give him the prize money for sinking a Portuguese pirate that he can claim at Resurrection.'

'But sir! That sloop, surely, was no pirate.'

'Aye, but he will say it was; and hand over its cargo, which is worth two times nothing, as proof of his devotion.'

'So our pirates are paid for hunting foreign pirates?'

'Oh, indeed! Though for the most part, the rogues work hand in hand, whatever their nationality. 'Tis only the smaller foreign buccaneers the big ones kill or, as in this case, lesser vessels not piratical at all.'

While I wondered at this, I found myself sorrowing that we should not see St Laughter; for much as I fear'd it, I had thoughts of Priscilla on it, and of my child. But casting these thoughts out (for they seemed vain), I said to the merchant, 'But does Nayle not fear the greater powers in Resurrection?'

'Lad,' said the chandler, smiling shrewdly, 'where there is power there is danger, but there is also greater protection for he who knows how to earn it.'

'But will Nayle not be anxious lest, at Resurrection where our fleet must be, they set out after him, once you merchants are all put ashore?'

The chandler laugh'd. 'Oh, there is a procedure in these matters, as you will see,' said he.

This procedure I was able to admire when at last we hove into sight of the island grac'd by the English capital of the Caribbean. At a fair distance, two of the merchants, younger men, and two of Nayle's crew, were put into the long boat to sail ashore. When they should return with the full ransoms, their fellows would be released as well. I wondered that Nayle did not fear they would sail back not with gold, but weapons. But the rope chandler (who was losing patience with one so doltish in these matters as I seemed to him) explained to me that on any sign of treachery, the merchants would instantly be slain. But there was more to it than that. In many of their dealings, both personal and commercial, the traders had learned to rely far more on the pirates, who were local men well acquainted with all their practices (here the chandler wink'd), than they did upon the navy; which, in the first place, was so often not there at all when it was needed, and, if it was, anxious only for mighty battles and great glory. And besides, the navy (whose pretty ships and uniforms the merchants paid for with their taxes) despised the traders, though they did not the planters, who were gentlemen as they. 'It is for this reason,' he concluded, 'that many of us prefer to trade in the island France. For if it is true that we are foreigners there, we are less encumber'd by the regulations of the French, than we would be helped in Resurrection by the succour of our government.'

The deputation was ashore a night and day, and did not return until next afternoon, by which time the merchants, tired of rum and dice, were almost rebellious. The long boat towed another; and this, I was told, was so that the merchants could sail off alone, without any of Nayle's crew, who might otherwise be seized on shore once the merchants had their freedom.

The gold brought by the delegates conformed, it seemed, to all that Nayle had required; and the farewells, if not hearty, were those of men who well understand the old adage of honour among thieves.

Diana, as queen of this little assembly, made to step off first into the boat; but Nayle begged her to let him get 'the old men' (as he put it) first safely stow'd. As soon as they were, he cried to his crew, 'Cast them off!' which the men, with a great heave, did; and when the boat seemed to tarry, as if still waiting for Diana, the Mate, on a word from Nayle, ran to the old cannon which, when those in the boat saw it pointed, caused them to sheer fast off.

The rage of Diana was wonderful to behold, and I thought she would pierce the deck with all her stamping. But Nayle, waiting till her screams and imprecations had in part abated, drew her aside from earshot of the crew, and said to her, 'Sure but, Miss Newbury, you must understand I cannot release you till I have laid hands on my treasure.'

'Villain! The boy will lead you to the slaves who took it!'

'Aye, lady: but consider. You also know of its existence. And, saving your honour, there is no man – or woman – in the world I can trust to keep silence till I have found it.'

'Your treasure! What is your treasure to me, if it exists, indeed!'

'To you, perchance nothing. But to many a man in Resurrection, everything, if they should hear of it, and think to try and take it from me. It has been stolen once; and now I am near to finding it again, I cannot risk a second time to lose it.'

Then she, in all her fury, brought up her fiercest weapon. 'But I am the daughter of a Planter!'

'Aye,' said Nayle, 'I know. And I regret I must detain you for that reason, since I do not wish to incur their animosity. But in such a case, I must.'

'The merchants will tell them that I am aboard!'

'Mayhap; but I do not believe, Miss Newbury, that the merchants love and respect the planters as greatly as you suppose.'

In vain did she scream and expostulate, calling Nayle names such as no maiden ought (at which he smil'd slightly), and crying out to the fast disappearing boat. And 'twas not till she broke away and tried to leap in the sea that Nayle called for her to be seized, and she was dragg'd away swearing vengeance on him, and upon mankind.

The Witch

THE MORE I reflected on my condition, the more it seemed to me that if it had perils, it had safeguards. For clear it was that, without me, Nayle could never find Daniel nor Bandele, because he knew them not; so that any danger to me could only arise (either from Nayle or from the ravishers of his treasure) if I ever found them; and until then, I was secure. True, Diana, now he had kidnapp'd her, also knew the two slaves; but it was not likely she would see them before I did — indeed, less so, if Nayle kept her even closer watch'd on board than I.

And besides, had I not wanted to serve with Nayle, to escape the dangers to me on the English islands? Judge of my dismay, then, and amaze, when Nayle had me brought into his cabin, and said, very calm, that I was to go ashore that night in Resurrection.

'But do you not fear, sir,' I said, trying to look sarcastick at him, 'that I may try to 'scape you?'

'No, boy,' said he. 'What I fear is rather that you might escape while I am not on my ship: for, you see, I too must go ashore in Resurrection.' He paused. 'And since you are the apple of my eye, you must accompany me, boy, chained. For it is as my slave that you shall go, my wrist clamp'd firmly to your ankle. You will pardon this indignity, I know.'

'I am surpris'd, sir,' said I, 'that you, illustrious buccaneer though you surely are, have yourself no fears ashore.'

To this he answered only by a mighty whack across my head with his telescope, so that I scarce felt the chains put about my feet; and came only to my senses when, in the long boat, we were approaching shore, though at a discreet distance from the harbour. Despite my pains, and fears of an island with courts and judges in it, my strongest emotion was one of curiosity as to what might be the purpose of Nayle's visit to this place; from which prudence, so I supposed, should invite him speedily to depart.

We beached under the cottages beyond Resurrection, which were neat and squat, but without the dazzlement of Avenir. The Captain mutter'd to his sailors, then calling me and dragging on the chain, he set off inland as if on a path known well, for it was shrouded. In the midst of a loneliness he stopp'd, jerking my foot so I stagger'd, and said in a low voice, 'Boy, consider!'

'What, sir?'

'How may you find two needles, that is two slaves, in a haystack, that is the Caribbean?'

'Indeed, I know not, sir, and have greatly wondered how you mean to do it.'

'One thing we know of or, at any rate, can guess. If they have gold, they wish to spend it. That means no deserted Cay, but a populated island.'

'So far, so good, sir.'

'Not a British island, since they are escaped. Then which?'

'If I were to guess, I would hazard an island ruled by those people who hate us most.'

'Well said, boy! So I have also reasoned. And thus I conclude, the island must be Dutch.'

'They like us less than all the others?'

'Aye, for two reasons. First, they are more like us than to the Spaniards, Portugese or French; and second, they are more recent here, and all upstarts hate their kind.'

'You are still left with a wide choice of islands, Captain.'

'Or is it the mainland, perchance? For the Dutch are established, like ourselves, in parts of El Dorado.'

'I hear 'tis vast, sir.'

'True: and that is the purpose of our visit here tonight.'

Seeing his pale face, with its spectacles glinting in the moon, I wondered fearfully if he might be struck by some insanity. I held my peace, and he said, speaking low, 'You are a Scot, boy. Do you believe in magic?'

'I know not, sir.'

'Nor I. But here on the islands, the natives do. And certain it is, they have some rare apprehensions . . .'

'But that is to believe in them yourself, sir.'

'Mayhap . . . But I am taking a sorceress on our voyage. And I shall hearken to her dreams, as well as to my reason.'

'She will come freely with you, sir? And if she does, will a native betray a native's secrets to you?'

'To this woman, in the past, I have given the two things most precious: her life, and her liberty from slavery. I shall also give her gold.'

'And how is she named, sir?'

'Mrs Obidiah. Come!'

The witch lived in a small, neat hut around which a multitude of cats prowl'd silently. To the Captain's knock, she opened readily enough, and boldly, greeting him (as I suppose witches are fain to) with the declaration that she had expected him. On me she bestowed only one hard long glance, and mutter'd a prophecy, or curse, or perhaps a benediction;

then seated us beside a fire on which she was roasting what seemed, and smelt, to be nothing more magickal than a fowl.

While the Captain unfolded his business to her – the thought of a wild dash round the Caribbean ocean seeming not to surprise her in the least – I examined this *obeah*-woman more attentively. Her chief peculiarity was that, had one not been told if she were man or woman, it would have been hard to determine which. Nor was her dress a help in this, for she wore none, save for a strip across a breast of dubious dimensions, and a cloth on her loins which could have hidden much or little. She listened without interruption to Nayle's story and then, turning to me, told me to describe Daniel and Bandele to her. When I had done so, she pronounced, with an immediate conviction, that the fugitives were at El Dorado.

This startl'd me, and the Captain too; for he had said nothing to her of his conjectures. Though reflection persuaded me that the witch could have reached this conclusion by the same powers of reasoning as we; and that after all, hers was but a guess, as ours had been. Yet the speed and certainty of her declaration were impressive.

Then, as if she were setting off to the village to buy split peas, she said only, 'Come!' and opened the door onto the night. I noticed the cats had all vanished. We made our way in silence back to the boat, Mrs Obidiah leading – indeed, it seemed, taking over the command. As we embark'd, there was a thunder clap.

I slept on the voyage back to *Scorpion*, despite a rocking, and was so weary I had almost to be hauled up on deck. Nayle had unlock'd my chain, but gave orders it was to be shackl'd to a rail beside the cot that was put in the Mate's den upon the stern. I prayed that night, for the first time since I had been made a slave.

And so we sailed due south to the Equator, toward the southern part of the Americas. I was not treated ill, and save for small tasks the Mate bestow'd on me, left to my own devices; and now we were so far from land, left unshackl'd, for Nayle did not think me desperate enough to leap into the sea. Diana held little converse with me or, indeed, with anyone, save for Mrs Obidiah: toward whom, from the sorceress's first appearance on the ship, she manifested a curious kind of condescending amity. Perhaps this was just the natural alliance of two women among men; but it seemed also that kind of understanding which two human creatures, in all fundamentals hostile, seem strangely to achieve. For to Diana, I think Mrs Obidiah was just one more *Mammy*, or old black female slave, which are the only kind the Planters treat with any decency, though roughly. While to the Sorceress, or so I guessed, Diana was a petty tyrant, entirely hateful, but whom it suited her to humour. As for Nayle, he spent much time with charts and musings, as if all his dreams were gold. The crew grew restless; for being all island men, they liked not long days without sight of land; nor, I suppose, since they were pirates, no chance for piracy.

This uneasy peace was shatter'd by an event heralded, one torpid evening, by a wild scream from the women's cabin, of which we were all soon to learn the cause. Diana, lying there alone in a half naked sweat (for it was stifling), had been peeped at through a crevice by the bombardier, a Londoner, the great manipulator of the cannon. Alas for her modesty – and the poor fellow's life – Mrs Obidiah was away cooking: her constant business in the galley, for she declared the ship's food uneatable, justly enough, and was a greedy witch. Seeing Diana thus unprotected, and fired with lusts usual to deprived seamen in the tropicks, the Cockney had burst in and tried to ravish her; earning only a great kick from Diana in his privies, and a smack on the pate with a frypan of burning hen from Mrs Obidiah, before being haul'd off by the Mate in a triple agony to face the just wrath of the Captain.

Yet Captain Nayle was mild about it, the more so, perhaps, because of the fellow's failure, and he ordered a mere hundred lashes. But this drove Diana to a frenzy, and she demanded death; which Nayle refusing (in terms as of dismissal to a child), she plucked a knife out of the Mate's belt, and stabb'd the poor Cockney in the belly; who fell bleeding with a great groan. Such of the crew as saw this murmur'd angrily, and Nayle, telling the Mate to fling the corpse into the sea, commanded the rest about their business, and summoned into his cabin the murderess, the sorceress and me.

He soon silenced Diana, who had fallen into a hysterick weeping, and said 'twas in part his fault, since he had not explained clearly to the crew that the young woman was inviolate. 'They would have understood,' said he, 'and respected it, had I carried her to my cabin. But I have promised this young woman that, once the two slaves are found, I shall return her immaculate to her father.'

'Aye, 'tis fear of my Father that protects me, not your honour, for you have none!' cried Diana, and Nayle did not deny this.

'This like a blood-clot mix-up,' observed Mrs Obidiah sagely. 'An' me, Captin, I see only one wise answer to it arl. The girl mus' get like marry.'

We all stared at her.

'Yes, Captin!' she declared. 'I know my people, an' half you crew is slave. Let they see a weddin', and they keep control of their emotion.'

'But 'twas not,' I ventured, 'an escaped slave who was the culprit.'

'Bukra man jus' the same,' the witch said to me disdainfully. 'Once they see she Mrs Someone, they more sensible, that is,' she added, half in a mutter, 'if Bukra man ever got any sense.'

'And to whom,' said Diana, with a glare like a thunderbolt, 'do you propose my hand be given?'

'To he,' said the witch, pointing at me.

Diana let out a horrid cackle. 'And who,' she enquired, 'will perform this ceremony?'

'He do,' said Mrs Obidiah, pointing to Nayle. 'Captin on he ship got a right to marry, good as priest.'

There was a silence.

'Miss Newbury,' said Captain Nayle, 'there may be something in this . . . stay, stay, I pray you . . . for though, if we continue as we are, I can command my crew to respect your person, and punish them if they do not, you must please remember they are pirates, whose discipline is not that of a common seaman. Nor, if others seek to behave as did the youth you have unfortunately slain, can I whip my entire crew, or a large part of it.'

'You are their Captain!'

'True. But because a pirate captain must make unusual demands upon his crew — among others, that they accept the risk of being hanged — he cannot punish them unless all manifestly feel this to be just, and in accord with the accepted codes of piracy.'

'If you cannot protect me, I see not how this boy can.'

'Honey, is the principul will protec' you,' said Mrs Obidiah. 'An' this boy ear the only person possible. Cos you see, Captin Nayle cannot be the bridegroom and the priest as well, now, can he?'

Diana glared at us, then let out a laugh. 'Oh, very well,' she cried. 'And it is well understood, Captain Nayle, that this ceremony has no meaning, legal or physical, except to curb a crew you yourself cannot control.'

Nayle bowed his head. 'Then that settle,' said Mrs Obidiah. 'The Captin perform at sun-up, the crew like guest, me bridesmaid, an' the Mate can stand witness for this ear boy.'

Everyone smiled.

'No,' I said.

'Oh!' said Diana. 'Oh – ho!' She looked at me with a mock'd affection. 'And I thought you *loved* me so, little slave!'

'Yes. And if ever I marry who I love, 'tis I who will choose, not others who will tell me.'

'Well!'

'Boy, you real obstinate. Me beginnin' to tink you got some black blood in you somewhere.'

'Come, boy,' said Nayle. 'You had better think of this.'

'And so,' said I, 'had all of you. For unless you force me to it at dagger's point, which will surely defeat your purpose when the crew see this is no marriage, I will only accept freely on one condition. And that is, if I am married, Mrs Obidiah moves out of my wife's cabin, and I move in.'

With this I walked out of the door, feeling mightily pleased with myself, tho' I regretted it at night. No more was said of all this in the morning. Diana was locked into her cabin, guarded at all times by the old Mate, or Mrs Obidiah, and only allowed out on deck in their close company. All three grew daily more enrag'd, Nayle sour, and the crew mutinous; and so we sailed into sight of the distant mountains, majestick on the southerly horizon, of El Dorado.

The Dutch

THERE are places in our World – and few, tho' it be so vast –
that exercise on human minds a special fascination. Of Africk
and the Orient I can say little, but in the Caribbean, the
country around the Orinoco, which we call Guyana, is such a
one. The Spaniards named it Golden, and when they were
beckoned across the Andes to the Incas, the English were
lured there in their turn; though often finding only misfortune, as did Ralegh. Coming from the islands, it seems
another world: so splendid and remote, with huge mountains
and fierce rivers in a continent that even now is scarcely
known.

All life – I mean all the life Europeans brought there –
clings to a fringe beside the sea. The islands, even the largest,
can be penetrated and even mapped. But in Guyana, who
knows what happens a few score miles inland? And of those
who discover, how many have returned to tell? The only
certainty is doubt; and the kings of this country are still the
Caribes, who, in the islands, have half vanish'd.

On these same islands, nature has solved the problem of
frontiers which, in their homelands, so perplexes Europeans;
for if you can seize an island, you seize it all. But in the
Guyanas, so huge and uncharted are the territories, that the
old fondness for squabbles over frontiers returns. At the
present, the Hollanders hold least – though the greater parts
the others say they 'hold' are half a phantasy, since in most

tracts claimed by France or England in their Kings' names, no Frenchman or Englishman has yet set his feet.

As we near'd this doubtful paradise, the crew all grew more sprightly. The black slaves chanted, the white wrestled, Mrs Obidiah told fortunes free, and Captain Nayle changed his broad-cloth into yellow ducks. Only Diana stayed morose, and sat in the prow, frowning and biting at her nails. But before we sailed in among the Dutch, where reason and magic both told us we might find the fugitives (and the gold), I determin'd on a last parley with Diana; and took advantage of a short absence of the Mate (who had climb'd up aloft to survey the coast) to sit on the deck beside her.

'Hearken, Diana,' I said to her, she making mien not to hear me. 'Here is our last chance, if we wish to, to escape from Nayle. He does not know the Dutch; and has no plots and intelligence with them like those he had upon the islands. Therefore, if we can but get off this boat, we can throw ourselves on their mercy, and they will help us.'

'Faugh! The Dutch!' said she.

'And they are Protestants,' said I, 'and so must be honest people.'

'Protestants!' quoth Diana.

'And most of all – consider! Why do we battle, you and I? Without us, Nayle can do nothing: only we know Daniel and Bandele, and we have but to defy Nayle together, to be masters of his destiny.'

'And he with an armed crew of ravishers?'

'I beg you to think!' cried I. 'What advantage can there be to us in any discovery of the slaves, or of the gold? If these should happen, how can they help you and me?'

'They will not help you,' said she, 'for Nayle, having done

with you, will slay you. Me it will help because once he has his treasure, I shall be restor'd to safety; and besides, as to the treasure, I shall see I get some part of it.'

'Your head,' cried I, 'is so pack'd with your own conceit, that you do not see the danger you are in – nor that I, in this predicament, am the only true friend that you possess.'

And now came upon us Mrs Obidiah, fresh from her triumphs of telling fortunes to the crew, which Diana sought to persuade her to do for us as well. 'Hé, but that be the trouble, you know,' the sorceress exclaimed. 'Cos me, when I read the bones, I tell nuttin but pure troof. Nuttin else at arl. But mos' customer, you see, they want to hear pretty story, but that me too honest a one to do.'

'Bring out your bones!' Diana commanded.

This, after a dark glance, the witch did, from the band about her copious middle. She shuffled round the brown'd lumps, muttering and rolling around her eyes, and it was a sort of triumph to her that even in daylight on this deck, with the sun beating on us, she contrived to conjure up a kind of darkness. Then she looked up at us with a beam, and cried, 'You fortunit, you know! Cos here, plain as an angel arse, it say you bot' get eggsackly what you hopin' for!'

'And what is that?' said Diana.

'Riches and glory! And you boy – what you want? Is salvation!'

'Aye,' said I.

'Ha! Well, you bot' get what you wish. Now, let we try Mistah Nayle!' She shuffled the bones again upon the deck, but a foot kick'd them awry, and we saw Nayle above us, frowning mightily. 'Come with me, boy,' he said. 'And you, Mrs Obidiah, your secrets are only for my ears, remember!'

In his cabin, Nayle told me to sit down, took a turn or two, then asked me, 'Can an honest lad like you have any reliance in a pirate?'

'Why, no,' said I.

He nodded. 'Boy,' he began, 'I need your help, and cannot force it from you, and you know this. So, to persuade you, I must earn this trust from you.' He paused. 'The discovery of my treasure,' he continued in a low, grave voice, 'is of more import to me than you may imagine. For it is not only gold. No. I am now, boy, in my fifties; and cannot remain a pirate chief forever, the more so as younger rivals are emerging.' He frowned. 'Besides which,' he went on, 'if I read the signs aright, the art of piracy itself will not endure much longer in these waters.'

I believe the Captain felt I should lament this misfortune with him, so I screw'd up a look of sympathy.

'So,' he proceeded, 'this is my decision: or, should I say' (he smiled a little), 'my hope. When I secure my treasure, I shall pay off my crew honourably, and myself retire to some commerce in the British part of the Guyanas. For there, if I have no friends, I have no enemies.'

'Can I believe all this, Captain?' I could not forbear to enquire.

'Upon my word, lad!' he cried most solemnly. 'Now – as to you. I make you this promise. Help me freely to recover what is mine, and I shall set you up decently, here among the Dutch, where you, too, can embark upon a life unsullied by your past.'

'And Diana?' I said.

'I shall put her on ship to St Laughter, or where she wishes: unharm'd, and sufficiently rewarded.'

'But Captain,' said I. 'Forgive me, but I have no surety of what you say.'

He gazed at me sadly. Then, rising solemnly, he went to a chest, rummag'd in it, and took out a tatter'd drapery which, when he unfolded it, I saw to be the dreaded Jolly Roger.

'This emblem,' said he, 'which is sacred to our craft, is not used any longer in these oceans. Where once, in our palmy days (which I happily remember as a lad), the sight of it struck terror in all hearts, it now, if display'd by any of our fraternity, has more the effect of bringing trouble and dangers on our own heads. Yet,' he said, raising it on high, 'to us it remains holy: sanctified by the blood of every gallant pirate who has perish'd in the Caribbean seas!' He now placed it on the table and, laying his hand upon it (with his fingers curiously cross'd in what, I supposed, must be some cabalistick buccaneering sign), he said to me, 'Boy, on this flag, and on my life, I swear to you!'

'Swear what, sir?'

He looked vex'd an instant, then said, 'All that I have promised.'

I put out my hand, that was at once enfolded in his strong and larger one. 'Captain Nayle,' I said, 'you have the word of a Scotsman that I shall do all I can to bring you peace!' And murmuring a Calvinistick prayer (which was, of truth, the multiplication tables 13 times 13), I raised my hand in salute, bowed to him, and departed.

On this part of the Dutch coast, there is no harbour: the vessels must lie out anchored in the shallows, and small boats put by to carry in their cargoes, or their crews. This we discovered by nosing in, for the Captain's charts, it seemed, did not extend this far. Bolder spirits than the Dutch might have planted a harbour further to the west where, we had spied, a wide river, seeming navigable, burst into the sea with little islands. But the Hollanders had preferred this settlement upon mud flats: which, even from our ship, we could see to be a trailing squalor.

The Captain went ashore, and took with him two crew, leaving the Mate master of the *Scorpion*. Through ill knowledge, we struck near the shore where the sea was shallowest, and had to leap out (save for Nayle holding the tiller) and drag the boat through half mud and sand up to the beach: this with a sun like I had never felt, and each halo'd in mosquitos. Leaving the crew to guard our boat (and promising to bring them rum, for we were running short on board), Nayle and I set off inland, and ere long tumbled into a sort of highway, or chief thoroughfare, which forms the artery of this horrid place, that is called Lettop.

We found it hard to encounter any Authority, for most of the huts and warehouses were lock'd (true, it was just after noon), and where we could find inhabitants, if they were slaves they would not reply, and if Dutch, gabbl'd in a surly jargon the Captain knew not. Till inspir'd, as 'twere, by Providence, I perceived a little church, and knocked upon the hut beside it. From it emerged, blinking in the heat, a stout man of middle years who knew some English. He said he was Pastor Nieuwenhuis, and that we might come in and speak with him free from the blaze.

He asked us our business, and now Nayle, putting up his gravest air, said that he was a trader in woods who hoped he might find some mahogannies if he ventured up the rivers. The Pastor shook his white head at this, and said to the Captain, '*Mijnheer*, you must be prudent in those rivers.

Mahogannies you may find; but also woods less desirable, I mean from blowpipes. For these the Caribes use, with venom'd darts, on those who venture too far up inside their sanctuaries.'

'But are not the Caribes well subdued?' the Captain asked.

'On the coast, yes: for truth to tell (and God rest their pagan souls), we have slaughter'd them here entirely. But though we have brought slaves here, I mean Africans, and laid out plantations, we have few soldiers to protect us, for our Government is tight-fisted. Or, in justice to them, I might say all our Dutch enterprise flows into the East Indies, leaving but little for the West.'

'But why,' enquired Nayle, 'do you not make slaves of the Caribes?'

Here the Predikant half smil'd, half sighed. 'But we have tried!' cried he. 'For why should we ship Africans this far when Caribes are thick upon the ground as snakes?' He peer'd at us both with his brows raised. 'But 'tis of no avail!' he said despairingly. 'Chains, whips and torturings mean nothing to them: rather than labour, the cowards prefer death!'

'Why, then, they are quite useless!' Nayle exclaimed.

The Predikant looked sage. 'No, not entirely,' he declared. 'For they love fighting, and pretty uniforms, and many have been conscripted by us. But we can only use them safely against our slaves: for if we attack the Caribes, even of other tribes, they grow treacherous, and cannot be relied on.'

Nayle, turning diplomat, now asked the Pastor if there had been any new arrivals recently – not from the Netherlands, he meant, but from the islands to the north? And in particular, had the Pastor knowledge of any blacks, calling themselves freed slaves, who had seemed rather richer than was usual with such people?

'For such matters,' Pastor Nieuwenhuis replied, 'I had better send you to the Intendant, who is representative of the House of Orange here, and has more knowledge of such matters than would I. For I, sir, am a man of God, not commerce.' The Captain thanked him, and said he hoped the Pastor would accept a small offering for the poor, which he agreed to, saying, 'Alas, sir, in this young colony we are all poor, though rich in spirit. For who can doubt that God has brought us here to win souls from the Devil and the Catholics.' And as we blinked out of the hut, he waved his hand tenderly over the muds of this bedraggl'd Promised Land.

To reach the palace of the Intendant, we had to hire donkeys for it was some miles off, and the roads knee-deep in mud. The Pastor pointed out the way which, as is said seemingly in every nation, 'we could not miss'. Yet this we did: for the road vanished into sugar fields, where a few slaves hack'd listlessly, and a warm stench rose from a net of ditches. For Lettop is sited, by the genius of its founders, upon a quagmire that is the accumulated silt brought down by streams that still trickle underneath. This makes the soil rich, but not the gaiety of the inhabitants.

At length we encountered a warrior, a Hollander, whose zeal to arrest us was our salvation. For he ordered us, musket pointing, along a track that brought us out at length before a kind of curious Dutch box, made of bricks imported from the distant Polders. After delays, and peerings at us by unshaven sentries, we were taken to the presence of the Plenipotentiary of the Netherlands.

This was a lean man with a fanatick glare, eyes like blue marbles, and a skeletonick frame. He claim'd no English, tho', by the intelligence of his stare, I believe he knew a little;

but address'd us through a fat young mulatto, all sweat and eager servility.

As to the mahoganny, said this functionary, we might sail up river if we wished, and the Intendant would offer us loyal Caribe troops as guides, for whom a fee must each be paid. On all shipments outward of the trees, a toll of one guilder would be due per stick (he meant a trunk). The duty for lying on the roads, out at sea as we did at present, was fifty guilder; and for entry in any stream, but twenty-five. Stores and weapons we could buy in Lettop from government marts, subject to tax of 200 per cent *ad valorem*, for these were scarce, and not offered to traders save as a favour. On the other hand, if we returned from the inland part successfully, we could have five cents for every Caribe head brought back (but only males), and ten cents for any living one of either sex.

All this had but scant interest to the Captain, but he was a patient man; and came now to his chief topick, as to whether His Excellency had knowledge of any escaped English slaves. 'For,' said Nayle, 'in addition to trading here, I have been asked by our government to try to track these fugitives, for they wish them brought home, and hanged as an example. I need not add, Excellency,' he concluded, 'that should our esteemed Dutch friends yield any up to us, a handsome recompense will fast be made.'

But when this was translated, the Intendant grew mightily vexed, and cried in a Dutch torrent that we insulted him, by calling him a slave-dealer; and that if the English could not control their slaves this was not surprising, for their behaviour shew'd they could not control themselves either; and with that he rose, and stalk'd out, without any of the courtesies habitual among Europeans.

The mulatto, waiting till he was gone, sighed and smiled, and said, 'There is one who might tell you this, whose name I could, of course, impart to you.' He looked meekly at the Captain, who handed him a coin; and, when the fellow waited, eyes lower'd, handed him fretfully some more. 'You should call,' said the mulatto, 'on the expert on all matters concerning slaves, who is Mijnheer Blockx. Ask for him anywhere in Lettop, and you will be directed to the proper place.'

At this he bowed away without further useful explanation, and all we could do was return to our donkeys and ride back to the town; which we did in a great jolting heat, Nayle cursing the Dutch for blockheads the whole journey. On the beach, we found our boat abandon'd, but still secure: and the seamen we unearth'd at last inside a rum shop, where they lay snoring, and we had to drag them to the shore and, since the wind had fallen, row ourselves out to the ship. Ever and anon Nayle kicked the drunkards, adding ten lashes to their sentence each time they groaned.

As we came closer to the *Scorpion*, Nayle was much annoyed to see shore craft tied up beside, which he had most strongly forbidden; and he half rose in his boat, as if to call for men to haul aboard the drunkards; but paused transfixed when, from the ship, we could hear great shouts and clamour like a revolution. Drawing his pistol, and crying, 'Row, boy!' Nayle stared ahead alert; and I could see by his furious glare that his pirate's honour was at stake, and his love of his dear ship, and that he was no coward. We reached the side unobserv'd, and clamber'd cautiously up.

Upon the deck, the whole crew was assembled, waving and cheering in a high excitement. And in their midst, we saw Mrs Obidiah, now naked, and plainly reveal'd to be in truth a woman. She was at the very paroxysm of a rustick dance and, as we stepp'd on deck, quite amazed, she flung out her arms and cried, 'Now which of you big boy be the nest? I hope good, cos I ain't seen nuttin like I expectin' from a pirate!'

At this the Cook, a fellow I think from Yorkshire, and of the dimensions of an elephante, hurl'd himself naked upon the sorceress, and roll'd with her upon the deck; their grunts encouraging the pirates to a frenzy. But crying, 'Od's tooth!' the Captain leapt among them, laying about him with the flat of his cutlass, and discharging his pistol in the air; at which the crew fell back a little, and one or two pert slaves from Lettop, that had boarded the ship from their canoes to sniff the spectacle, sprung overboard and away. But the amorous pair, so intent were they upon their purposes, scarcely noticed the affray, taking the din, no doubt, as a general proof of admiration; and not till nature itself had led them to disengage, did they sit up, panting, to confront the indignant Captain.

'Lordy lord!' said Mrs Obidiah. 'That cook know how to roast, boil, fry an' stir a stew.'

'To your feet, shameless hussy!' Nayle cried. 'Mate! Throw the cook in irons!'

But no Mate came forward, and Mrs Obidiah, rising heavily, said, 'Mate lock up in Miss Diana cabin.'

'What!'

'Now, don' go get excite, please, Mistah Nayle. He not jus' lock up theer, he *tie* up, too.'

'What is this, woman?'

'Well, he tink this performance not suitable for she to see, the young lady, so I say to he is best to stay inside thear to proteck her. But in case he peep out an' get excite, I grab he, and tie he to her bed.'

'Which villains helped you?'

'Helped me? Captin, I can tie two men with one hand!'

'You will be punished for this, woman! Put on your garments! Men – to your duties!'

The Captain glared around and they slunk off, though smacking their lips and chattering. Mrs Obidiah picked up her two inches of cloth from the deck, and wrapped them round her person modestly.

'But Captin,' she said patiently. 'Wasn't you afraid some rape come on Miss Diana, cos they energies all bockled up? Well, see, I help you by I unbockle them.'

These sights and words seemed to have strange effeckts on the composed nature of Captain Nayle. After a minute's silence, and slapping of his sword against his twitching limb, he said severely, 'Come to my cabin, Mrs Obidiah.'

The Dealer

I HAD almost thought all order upon the *Scorpion* was disrupted; but here I did not yet know Captain Nayle. Nor how an officer, if he has guile, courage and confidence all greater than his men's, can redeem lapses that seem slipping into mutiny. Next morning, it was as if an Avenging Devil had descended on the ship. The Mate was cast down to seaman, a stern young Quartermaster rais'd in his place. The Cook had no lashes, lest the food get even worse, but lost an ear; though with that judicious injustice common to commanders, Nayle did not punish any other fornicator, but only the one who had affronted him by being seen. Some slaves were lash'd for no reason in particular, and two picked out, that had done nothing and despite their pleading, to be sold on shore. The whole crew were turned into chambermaids and made to scrub, paint and mend the ship, or sent into Lettop to heave heavy stores aboard. The punishment of Mrs Obidiah, the chief culprit yet most difficult for Nayle to discipline, was to be put on a fruit diet for several days; from which, wailing the while, she shrank visibly.

These proofs of his power seemed to confer on Nayle an added certainty that the fugitives, and the gold, were somewhere near. And though, without knowing at all why (I mean rationally), I shared his belief, I must admire his certainty, and his persistence. For me, all I had at hazard was my life: of prime import, certainly, but I had little else to distract me. But for Nayle, what was at stake also was his ship, his judgement and (if one may call it so) his whole career.

In pursuit of the hint offered by the Intendant's mulatto, and though we had but little faith in it, we were to go ashore in search of Mr Blockx. Diana, who was by now almost frantick with boredom and frustration, begged to be allowed at least to walk on land as well. But this Nayle denied her utterly; and by bribing the young Quartermaster, promoted Mate, by gold and threats (and also, I overheard, the pledge of bringing him a whore aboard that night), he told this stalwart to keep her lock'd up and closely guarded. And lest Mrs Obidiah, despite her diet of fruits, might succumb once more to setting an ill example, he carried her into the boat for shore as well: she complaining mightily of the heat, and shouting complaints to the dark idlers on the beach in her thick island accent which, to Nayle and me, was often a mere abracadabra (though the natives nodded at her jests).

To ask any in Lettop for the whereabouts of Mijnheer Blockx was to earn, if they were a slave, a surly look or, if a Hollander, a sort of snigger. The reason for this came into view when we learned that this Blockx was chief dealer in slaves along this coast. In the older colonies this trade, because demand and supply are fairly equated, and can be reasonably judged, is fairly stable; and while it is true the Planter aristocracy despises any trade, there is no special disgrace attached to that in human bodies.

But in the Guyanas it was rather otherwise. For here the plantations were so ill established, and precarious, that the demand for slaves was quite unstable; and further, few slave ships visited this coast, both because of the distance, and the uncertainty of any market. This meant a slave-trader in El Dorado must be a speculator which, in this connection, means a rogue.

The ingenious Mijnheer Blockx, so they told us in the rum shops (where he seemed much admir'd), has insured to some degree against the fluctuations of his trade by breeding as well as trading: not only did he buy slaves from Africa, but created a new Africa of his own. This has one curious effect. It is usual, in the islands, for the African culture in a slave – as speech, or pagan faith, or music and tribal customs – to be largely lost, even after one generation; so much are slaves from different regions hurl'd together, and so little encouraged to remember their lost bliss. But in Guyana, where Africans are bred as such, their old coherence may last much longer.

The present Blockx, the gossips said, was not the originator of this experiment in generation. We would find him a young fellow, for it was his old *grootvader*, and then *vader* – both no more – who were the creators of this South American Elysium. We would also see how his knowledge of the whole Guyana coast (that is, the English and French parts too) was un-rivall'd by anyone else's since he was the chief provider of limbs in all these areas. And it was for this reason, we divined, that the Intendant's mulatto had guessed Blockx would know of any strange motions among the slaves.

So we hired a bullock cart and drove out some six miles to trader Blockx's establishment: which was called, they said, *Uit Twee, Twintig*. We found it to be a small plantation, mostly of vegetables and some beasts, with slave tenements, and a neat white house over which flew a flag bearing Mijn-heer Blockx's emblem, $2 = 20$.

Mr Blockx was an affable young man, full of smiles even

when he discovered we were not buyers or sellers of his flesh, but curious and admiring visitors. He led us round his farm where the slaves of both sexes looked, I thought, by comparison with the dull desperation of the plantations, quite healthy, yet entirely listless: as if aware that to be bred as beasts is, if that were possible, an indignity even greater than to be made to labour like them.

The Captain, noticing they were not shackl'd, asked how Blockx prevented their escape.

'Ho!' cried Mr Blockx. 'Well, we have dogs. But if they run, where can they run to? In the village they would be known at once, and brought back in a twinkle. And if they run inland . . .' here Mr Blockx made a gesture as of mastication '. . . pop! the Caribes will eat them!'

'Now tell me,' said Mrs Obidiah, who had been pondering and gazing round about her. 'How you pair up these peoples? Boy pick the pussy he wants breed, or does you, or they all jumble up like fus come fus serve, and devil take the hindmost?'

'It is a problem!' Mr Blockx confessed – speaking as if not in reply to Mrs Obidiah (for a black can have no opinions), but to the Captain, or the Voice of Disinterested Enquiry. 'For take what precautions we may to mate the male and female of our choice, we are confronted here with an instinct even more powerful than fear, which is natural physical attraction. All we can do is to ensure, by strict segregation, that a selected female is allowed no commerce save with the chosen mate until conception is achiev'd. Once the female is fertilis'd, supervision is abandoned, for when we tried to enforce this, there were numerous murders.'

'And what type of product do you aim at?' asked Captain Nayle. 'One with strength, I suppose, chiefly?'

'We have three criteria,' said the breeder. 'Strength, obviously, as you have guessed, sexual potency, and . . .'

'How you test that? You use a scales?' the witch enquired.

'Any tendency to sterility in male or female can quickly be established, and the defective breeder eliminated from our farm by sale. Apart from that, it is a matter of matching up equivalent potencies. This is not, as you might suppose, a matter of equating similarities: cross-breeding between tribes of varied physical structures leads to the happiest results, and we are constantly experimenting.'

'And what is your third *desideratum*?' asked Captain Nayle.

'Why, intelligence!'

'Is that not dangerous?'

'Far from it. Stupid labour is lost labour. And if an intelligent slave is doubly frustrated, his rage takes the form, if properly disciplined and guarded, of additional energy.' He gazed at the superb and languid bodies around us with satisfaction. 'In fact,' he continued, 'you might even say we are creating here a kind of human perfection. Already, when you come to think of it, a first selection of the ideal labouring sire, or labouring dam, has been made, by our good friends the slavers, out in Africa. For depend upon it, if you are in this business, and you are offered a herd of captured warriors and their consorts on the Coast, you do not pick the dolts, the weaklings, or the impotent. A further perfection is attained aboard the slave ships, where any surviving wastrels are cast aside. And here, where we have time to proceed scientifically, we are in process of creating a type of African infinitely superior in all respects to the crude raw material of his distant country.'

'Me tink it digustin',' said Mrs Obidiah.

The dealer smiled. 'In Europe,' he said, 'we proceed on an equivalent principle, but clumsily and imperfectly. Thus, our aristocracy is inter-bred, and so, to a considerable extent, is there selective breeding among families dedicated to particular professions, as soldiers, sailors, farmers, even clergymen and lawyers! For mankind, since (unlike animals) it can breed consciously, should do so to achieve the most appropriate effects.'

'But in Europe, they have some freedom.'

'Yes, boy, alas they have: which means many inter-mixtures are imperfect. Our nobility, for instance, is sullied by many illegitimacies; and as for those classes where the union is quite haphazard, the most horrid freaks and lunaticks can be the consequence, as you must know. But here what we aim at is a creation both rational and humane: aye, humane, for on my farm there are few of the rigours to be found on a plantation – or even, I dare say, Captain, on your ship.'

'Aye,' said Nayle, though his face wore, to my surprise, a sort of supercilious disapproval. 'Aye, Mr Blockx, but even the slaves upon my ship, if they violate not discipline, can copulate as they will.'

'Blood seed, Captin, you outrageous!'

'Captain, there can be no degrees in slavery: it is absolute, or nothing. Once you accept that the slave has any right, other than to stay alive for the exact span of his effective labour, you undermine fatally the whole institution.'

Mrs Obidiah, who had been looking earthward, raised her head; and speaking not to Mr Blockx, but as if it were to her-self (or to the sky) said, 'Well, now, Mr Dutch, if I was governor of this ear surroundings, the fus ting I do is to abolish you. Becos what I would be saying to myself, is this.

If is one man six dog, he can control them, make them work, with whip, collar, and starvation. One man an' sixty dog, gets more perilous. One man six hundred . . . Well, I tink one day they dog hop up an' tear this man in bits an' eat he up.

'An' that, Mr Dutch, and Mr Nayle, and you too, boy, is goin' to be your puzzle. Becos to make these island and places rich, you must bring moah slave ear, or breed them, like this fellow. Must bring moah an' moah – can't ever stop. But one day come when they slave look around and say, "Why we not grab that whip? Why not tear off this collar? Why not we eat the food? An' why we not take this blasted man, this blood-clot, lean-arse, poor-prick, piss-colour, rag-'air, squeak-voice ghost, and do to he . . ." '

'Woman – enough!' Nayle said sternly. 'You will excuse her, Mr Blockx, and me, but she is a freed woman, and beside . . .' (and he whispered in the Dutchman's ear).

Mr Blockx, who had been looking with slight apprehension towards his slaves, that could not but hear Mrs Obidiah's penetrating oration, smiled slightly, and said, 'Oh, yes, the witches – they can be useful; but they should be whipp'd now and again, Captain, they should be whipp'd!'

The Captain nodded and, taking advantage of this introduction to the theme of our visit, asked had Blockx news of any rebellious slaves, or any seeming to have stolen property. The breeder reflected, then said,

'Captain, I have told you the Caribes are hostile to the slaves; and that is indeed true, since they regard all interlopers in their continent, however brought here, as their enemies. But further up the coast, as you will know, there is a river, called by us the Wilhelmina, since the Caribe name for it is unpronounceable. Now, this stream lies upon the frontier of our territory, and those claimed to the north by France, and in the upper reaches, by your people. A consequence of this division of authority – which, to the disadvantage of us all, leads to unseemly squabbles – is that the stream is a kind of no-man's-land, or everybody's; and consequently attracts any evil or disruptive element of our three colonies. It is thus on the Wilhelmina that one might expect to find any miscreants – 'scaped slaves, turncoat Caribes, even, I fear, exiled whites who fish in these troubled waters.'

The Captain, glancing at me, said, 'Step away a moment, lad,' and continued in close parley with the Dutchman. I approached Mrs Obidiah, who was attempting to make commerce upon the slaves, and offering them charms. But squatting upon their haunches, with their arms trailing, they looked back at the sorceress blankly.

'Lord, but these poor boys dumb,' said she.

'Nay, Mrs Obidiah. 'Tis surely that they speak Africk tongues, and therefore fail to understand you.'

'You's a bright boy,' she answered, 'but not so bright as that. Cos when an *obeah* woman speak, let me tell you, it ain't in any particular language. Is like universal.'

'If they understood what you said to Mr Blockx, and tried to act on it, all you would have earned them is a whipping.'

'You sure? Boy, if me was planning any kind of trouble for Mr Dutch Planters around ear, this farm is the fus place I come to for me voluntear.'

I glanced at the melancholy figures who, so resembling the men lock'd upon the slaver, had that far-off Africk look that distinguishes them from the sharp eyes of those born in the Caribbean; and one, in particular, who caught my eye, reminded me in memory of Bandele.

It was. I froze. Mrs Obidiah let out a sudden scream. 'Captin!' she cried. 'The ship! Out on she ship! Is Miss Diana!'

Nayle whirl'd around, and so did the Hollander, for from his bred slaves there now rose an enormous wail. He called out for dogs and overseers, while Nayle grasped the trembling witch who, eyes starting, would only exclaim, 'Back to the ship, Captin! Race, man, race – or she go gone!'

We tumbled into the bullock-cart, and thudded over the ruts back into Lettop. The Captain ran to our boat, we following, and as it put off, he gazed piercingly out upon the *Scorpion*, where all seemed, from this distance, still and calm. Nor were we greeted with any kind of dismay when we climbed up on deck, the crew seeming all resting, or about their business. Nayle hastened to Diana's cabin which was locked, and no answer coming to his blows, he called on two men to burst down the door.

Within, there was only the young Quartermaster, lying neat upon the cot, and naked. When he was pluck'd up, his head, limbs, and all extremities fell off, for he had been sliced neatly, then laid in place again.

The Captain seemed less surprised, even dismayed, than anyone. A glint shone in his eye, and he said quietly, 'They have betrayed themselves into my hands; for now I know they are here, and where they will go to; and the girl will reveal them to me, for alive or dead, her presence in Dorado can never be kept hidden.'

'Captin,' said Mrs Obidiah, 'I don' wish you bad, and so I tink you should sail home.'

'Sir,' said I, 'if they have stolen away Diana, it is to lure you to her.'

The Captain looked at us evenly. 'I know,' said he. 'They want my ship. I want my treasure. Each wishes for the other's life. So be it, and it is now that we shall learn the outcome.'

None had seen any marauders come aboard, nor Diana taken, all the crew swore. This smelt to me of treachery, despite their vehemence. But Nayle punished none, and put none ashore. Instead, he took on Dutch and Caribe soldiers, and replenished guns and stores. Only Mrs Obidiah was left behind, to be put on a boat back to Resurrection, and well paid. Neither Nayle, nor even she, said why. But I guessed it was because the Captain trusted her magic to bring him close up to his prey, but did not credit her loyalty any further.

And I had other guesses, that I was determined to essay on her. By pretext that she must take messages to Priscilla, should her ship pass by St Laughter (and also some little gold that I had come by), I tried to penetrate her secrets, if she had any: saying to her,

'Mrs Obidiah, I respect your magic: but may not a magician help his own spells a little?'

'What you mean, boy?'

'If Daniel and Bandele have indeed caused her to be taken, they must have known that she was on the boat, and where, and how guarded.'

'So?'

'So someone must have told them.'

'Boy, if you mean me, is the day she fled the first day in my life that I see Bandele.'

'But shore slaves have come out to the ship, and perhaps you spoke to them; or perhaps, too, when we landed on the beach before going to the breeder's farm.'

'Oh! You tink so?'

'So I guess . . . But of one thing I am not sure. Did Diana go freely when they came, and help them? For if she was ravish'd, the crew must have known and heard.'

'Boy,' she said, 'you got the wrong ideas entirely. These tings is right away up above your poor white head. No bukra ever understand *obeah*, I tell you. Hey! What you want Priscilla boy call, if he born now, an' livin'?'

'Absolem,' said I.

The River

IN ISLANDS, and island people, I think there is a kind of madness. I have noticed how, in my own country, Scotland, the Lowlander has a kind of sense and docility, whatever his defects; while the Hebridians show a wild kind of extravagance. My domine had taught me, I remember, that the European islanders, like Cretans and Sicilians, were also volatile; and of Irishmen, I do not need to speak. In the Caribbean, I had thought to notice a same kind of effervescence: a nervous restlessness, that can carry men (and women too) to an extreme pitch of passion.

It was thus that, as we sailed along the great coast of the Guyanas, the different spirit of the continent had on most of us an unaccustomed effect. I mean that in islands, man must feel big because he knows the land is small, and all he really respects at all, or fears, is the encompassing sea. But here, the land seemed just as vast, and we the smaller.

Our Captain had at first sailed north, away from the coast, as if he had abandoned his whole enterprise. But we soon discovered that he had another purpose. He wanted to remind his crew, and the new conscripts, that they were fiends, and he their master. Closer to shore, seamen may think, and do, of other authorities beside their Captain's; but on the high seas, they know there is nothing between mutiny and complete obedience. Besides, for Nayle's rehearsals, he clearly wished to be outside the chance report of craft putting in at the Guyanas.

He first sought out some smaller ships for the crew's refreshment in the art of piracy. On his earlier venture I had seen (I mean with the Portuguese sloop), the display had a kind of drab efficiency, without gusto. But now the cargo, or a ransom, interested him not at all, but only to instruct his men in cruelties, so that he could ask worse of them when at last we sailed into the Wilhelmina. I shall not relate the wanton tortures he caused his men to perform, though they were terrible and numerous; for to remind myself of them, is also to remember that I, too, and to my horror, took a taste to them like everybody else For it is in the nature of man, even the basest, that he cannot be cruel, and keep his sanity, unless it is through such a habitual familiarity that cruelty becomes but custom.

Nayle's further skill was to stir up the crew against each other, even though this caused some deaths, and many woundings. I wondered that none ever saw how, by giving satisfaction to their nastiest instincts, he won dominion on them. Yet perhaps they did see this, and welcomed it; for most men like to be ruled, and for another to free them from the heavy weight of holding any judgement of their own.

Lest any think that Nayle could not himself do what he ordered others, he personally performed, without any passion although expertly, some acts so monstrous that they had a kind of horrid splendour; so that even the crew cried out, or some of them. At this, as a kind of culmination to their perfection, he offered a prize of a gold piece to he on the ship who could devise the agony which should be greatest, yet last longest to the victim. This was won by a half Caribe from Lettop, and was inflicted on a Dutch trooper that had refused an abominable order, and for this had been condemn'd for mutiny. The lad survived three days as we sailed back toward

the coast, and might have suffered longer, had not the crew
begged Nayle to give the torturer his gold, and despatch the
boy, for the screams hindered them from sleeping.

Before we reached the estuary, Nayle summoned us for an
oration. I do not think the crew understood all he said, I mean
the words; but the sense was clear to them. And it was this.
They knew him, he said, and his reputation in forty years of
piracy. First on the *Scorpion*, he admitted, was himself; but
immediately after – and dear to him because he depended on
them utterly – came his crew. If he won rewards, they did,
and they knew this. The fortune he now offered them was the
greatest in his career. He did not know for sure if he would
find it; but if he did, they would be certain he had done so,
because he would share it equitably with each man of them,
according to his stature on the ship. One crime, and one only,
was forbidden them, as they knew; and that was any faltering
or treachery. To this, after a silence, there was a subdued
hurrah.

The entry to the Wilhelmina, despites its grandeur (for its
expanse is visible from the sea), was hazardous because of a
multitude of islets, or mud deltas, that encumbered it. Nor
were these charted, so that we proceeded slowly, casting lines;
till Nayle, sighting some Caribe canoes in a flotilla, and ordering his Lettop Indians to hail them, offered the natives rum to
guide us in, which they agreed to; but whether by accident
or misunderstanding, they landed us on a submerg'd drift,
where we must wait stuck fast for the tide turning at nightfall.

The Captain set a watch, and as a special precaution, for he
did not trust the Caribes (I mean, less than most), laid out the
ship's boats in darkness, at some distance, to watch if any canoe
might try stealthily to approach. Then, as if casually, he

summoned me to the stern, beyond his cabin, and looked across the estuary in silence before saying, 'Well, how are we to do it, boy?'

'We, sir?'

'Aye – we.'

'I know not, Captain, and indeed I have been wondering as to your intention.'

'Well, to find my treasure I must first find the slave Daniel. And what will bring him out of hiding, is my ship.'

'Sir, so you have told me. But what would he need with *Scorpion*, and what could he hope to do with it?'

The Captain rubbed the carved balustrade of the old ship fondly. 'In the Caribbean,' he replied, 'to earn wealth, and hence power, you must have one of two things, or perhaps both: land, or a vessel. Now, the slave cannot hope to be a landowner; but black pirates, former slaves, have not been unknown.'

'But if that were his intent, he could perhaps seize a smaller ship than yours, and safer.'

'A small ship were useless for piracy, and where we lie now, no large ships come. Nor can he venture to a more populous place, where gold can buy vessels, being a fugitive, and hunted; that he has fled here is the proof of it. So he must tempt me here: and I must tempt him down to me with *Scorpion*.'

'And so he would become a pirate! Then what need has he of your gold?'

Nayle turned and looked at me, as if examining his own mind. 'There was, boy,' he said at last, 'a Rising at the French island, where I took you. There have been others in these waters: small, dispersed, fitful, doomed and bloody. For what can chained limbs and minds do against our might? But perhaps there are slaves who still have dreams: for we must not forget, boy, that they come from Africa, a continent that has had many kings.'

'And they would seek to build a kingdom here?'.

'They would dream of it, perchance: and for this gold is needed, for men are not enough. Or so they may reason . . .'

'And they could do this, Captain?'

'No. Even with gold, with ships, with arms, it cannot happen. For a slave, boy, ceases to be a man: he loses our chief faculty, which is not just to strive, but to persist and win.'

I looked upstream into the overhanging night. 'Then you will not sail up the river to seek him, Captain?'

'Into his jaws, and in uncharted waters? No: I shall wait in the estuary. Sooner or later, he will come.'

I did not reply, for I was wondering if, in his belief that old *Scorpion* was the greatest treasure man could desire, the Captain was not yielding to an excess of love for it. Suddenly, his hand was upon my shoulder. 'Boy,' he said. 'You trust me?'

'Why do you ask this?' I cried. 'For you must understand, I cannot answer your question truthfully, without affront.' And indeed, I reflected, had I full trust in Nayle, I would not have hidden from him that I had seen the slave Bandele, or thought so.

'Aye, boy,' the Captain said. 'But you do not believe I mean you ill?'

'I must suppose so, sir,' said I.

'Well,' said Nayle solemnly, 'to prove to you my trust, I intend sending you up the river, without guards, and free, but with soldiers to protect you.'

'With what purpose, Captain?'

He placed his hand upon my neck again, and said, 'Lad, I know you have lost your heart to the girl Diana, and would wish to save her from the slaves if, indeed, she is with them, and still living.'

I said nothing to this so, pressing harder on my shoulder, he said, 'Well, boy?'

'Captain,' I said. ' 'Tis true I love Diana Newbury. 'Tis true also I would wish to bring her out alive. But I do not believe she has any fondness for me, or would show gratitude.'

I saw the Captain smile, but kindly. 'Women are various,' he replied. 'Restore her to her people, and you would be her hero.'

'Mr Nayle,' I said at last, 'I am young, and in love, but not quite a fool. You must have some other purpose in this offer.'

'Aye, boy.'

'It is for me to see Daniel.'

'Aye.'

'And say that you await him.'

There was a silence. Then, 'To say that, yes, and to say further: that I know he will never achieve his purpose unless he seeks to prevent me from achieving mine.' When I said nothing, he said gently (and with a kind of affection that I almost believed), 'Go and think on this, lad, and tell me. For it is useless to send you unless you go freely, with an honest promise to me of your return.'

Next morning .we escaped the drift, and coasted up cautiously into the estuary. It was a quarter mile across, with the current on the far, or eastward, side of it; and on the west, a sort of still pool, deep enough for anchorage, yet so far from shore that we could not be surpris'd by boats, and shot by arrows. Here the Captain anchor'd, and mounted constant watches. Caribes rowed out sometimes to look at us, but kept their distance. Some of their canoes set off up the river, which sight pleased the Captain, since it would bring tidings thither of our presence, as he desired. And when they returned again, and did not show any fight, he ordered his cannon on them, blasting wood and bleeding limbs into the golden stream.

Nayle said no more to me of his proposal that I should seek Diana. There had seemed to come over him, during the days we lay idle, but watchful, in the estuary, a kind of enormous patience, yet a calm certainty. One might think he was like a gambler, staking everything on a last throw: but no gambler could have been so placid. It was almost, indeed, as if Nayle, attentive yet serene, had become possessed by some kind of Revelation. And I thought of him, 'Well, this villain is a kind of Calvinist, since he believes firmly in predestination.'

As for me, all my thoughts were torn in two. It seemed that, ever since I had been summoned by destiny to St Laughter, I was doomed to belong to no sure party, possess no secure friend, be buffeted between every kind of interest and passion, having none left of my own. Seeking my interest, which was to escape out of all this, and try to begin afresh in some place where I was not punished perpetually for sins I had not committed, what should be my course of action now? For if I could never trust the wildness of the slaves, nor could I, when I examined his motives (or what I took them to be), trust the duplicity of a pirate either. So I took to prayer: but felt each day that the answer became fainter and more uncertain, so that I came at last to fear that my own predestination was to doom.

In this cloud of doubt and indecision, two feelings spurr'd me at last to action. One was, though my mind told me it was foolish, that I hoped to see Diana once again: for you must remember that I was a boy of seventeen, and that for all such, though they are become in most ways men (at any rate, in the Caribbean, where you must mature fast to survive), they may still have a kind of infatuation for a first love, however unworthy. The other reason for decision was a base one: it was that the boredom and menace in the estuary hung so heavy, that I preferred to its static torpor a movement in almost any sense. So I spoke to Nayle, and said I would go up the river.

He seemed not a bit surprised; in proof of which were the preparations which I found he had made for the expedition. A long boat had been armed and provisioned, and a crew of three others chosen. These were a Caribe rear'd by the Dutch, called Hendrickx; a 'scaped slave from the island they call France, whose name was Antoine; and an older English sailor (tho' he was perhaps not yet thirty) whom Nayle trusted specially, because he had taken this man, called Charles, onto *Scorpion* when he was but a boy. Nayle said that Charles was to be the leader of our party; but that he must hearken to my counsel as to whither we should go, and how proceed. For Nayle had a kind of faith that I would find Daniel: which, such was my superstition (or perhaps Nayle's dominion over me), I believed as well.

We advanced chiefly by sailing, but as the river narrowed, we must take to paddles. A double puzzlement was that the Wilhelmina, from this point upstream, splits into many channels some leading, as we found, to nothing, or else in great elipses back to the original stream. The other inconvenience was that the mud plains gave way to forest, and we were often overhung by nets of green, hiding the sky. The Lettop Caribe was useless to us, for he neither knew the course himself, nor could enquire of it from the natives, for these kept hidden.

As we camped one evening, the sailor Charles, ordering Antoine and Hendrickx to unload and cook, took me aside and said he thought we should leave the boat secreted, and proceed on foot. 'Consider,' said he. 'There are now mountains rising round us, and if there is any slave camp here, as the Captain supposes, it will surely be hidden from the river, and we shall never see it through the jungle; but if we climb up, at least we can get a view of it, for there was never a camp I knew of without smoke. Besides, it is clear the natives are watching out for us, but hidden along the banks; so that if we walk inland, we may come up behind them, and discover them.'

'But we cannot walk great distances and carry arms and stores,' said I.

'We shall not have to. You may be sure that if there is a camp at all, it will not be far from the coast. Escaped slaves would have no reason to go far inland, and every motive to go into the jungle only so far as protects them from pursuit and capture.'

'But in our boat, our own escape were easier, in case of danger.'

'On the contrary. Following the river, we are always visible for attack, and they may launch out boats behind us, to cut us off. But once inland, they will never know where we are.'

It may seem strange, even unbelievable, that we should think solemnly of entering a huge forest totally unknown to us, and where perhaps innumerable enemies lay hid. He who has doubts of this, can not have heard of the intrepidity that possesses Europeans in the Americas. Cortez and Pizarro, with a few hundred men, once conquered nations. And today,

two centuries afterwards, a European, and even one un-
distinguished, can still be sustained by this example, and show
rash courage. This is due, in part, to a superiority in arms, if
not in numbers; but also to a furious arrogance which, however repulsive in a human sense, can lead to acts of extra-
ordinary bravery. Indeed, in the whole sad story of the
conquest of the Americas, this wild fearlessness is the only
pure beauty we have brought.

So it was decided; the boat was hid, and we climbed upward, the Caribe in the van (he being forest-footed), then I,
next Antoine (whom we trusted least), and Charles watching
as our rearguard. The air grew colder, for in South America
the ascents can be so steep, as from the tropical to temperate
in a few hours. Also the jungle gave way to rocky tundra. We
reached an inferior summit, and stared out.

I had never seen anything on earth as beautiful. Scotland I
had thought glorious, as indeed the Highlands are; but beside
this Prospect, the memory of the glens seemed as of a toy
countryside for dolls. For here nature was not only wild, but
Olympian and serene. Mountains succeeded like waves of a
blue ocean, rising to the pink peaks of the Andes. A hundred
rivers twisted and glistened, like silver arteries in this huge
body. Overall hung a mist, shot through with shafts of light
extending miles. We also saw the smoke.

Charles was for hiding, caution, and a deft nocturnal approach. But I rebelled against this, for myself. I said there
could be no hope of stealing away Diana unless it was by her
will. And to persuade her, if I could, I had come to think the
fastest and only way was to invite capture and then, using the
arts of the defeated that slavery had taught me, see if I could
make of her an ally in her own theft. Charles thought this

folly, and forbade it. But I took advantage of their distraction
to leap into the bush and tear off down the hill. They did not
fire after me, perhaps by surprise, consideration, or fear of
revealing where they were.

Truth to tell, there had come over me a sort of madness, or
elation, due to the exuberance of the thin air on the mountain
and, even more, to a frantick belief that life which had
offered me such cramped miseries would here, at last, in this
surviving paradise, bring me a free joy. So I ran down like a
hare, or bird: leaping, almost flying and, when I had breath,
hallooing to the sky. This rapture fell into a stumble, and a
crack'd head; and the voice that greeted me when I awoke
was, 'Rise up, now countryman, we been expectin' you.'

In the forest, Bandele was a man. It was not just that the
squalor of slavery had fallen from him, but that in this noble
landscape, he seemed at ease. Caribes came with us, who did
not seize on me, though they walked holding their pipes
against any flight. But they all seemed in this lair too full of
confidence for much precaution.

We saw their encampment from a distance. It lay round
one of those hewn pyramids which the Red Indians, so the
Dons tell us, have built in many parts of the Central Americas,
and which are devoted to some pagan worship of the sun. This
one, which was salmon-coloured, was squat and seemed to be
ruinous, as if from this part of the Americas, the Caribe gods
had made away. As we drew nearer, I saw huts and some
larger broken buildings round it, made also of stone; and a
busy movement of the village population, which I noticed at
once had not that turgid, absent step of slaves, but a casual
briskness. These people seemed in part Africans, part Caribes;
which led me to suppose that Mr Blockx was less aware of

what went on inside his colony than he had pretended.

I was not afraid, because I was past fear: or, since no man can be truly that, I mean in a state of momentary fearlessness due to a sort of indifference that had come over me as to my fate. Bandele, though he did not seem hostile, walked as if in a cloud, and answered the queries I put to him with mumbles and nods that told me nothing.

On a field below the temple, they were drilling. I do not mean the chess-board exercises of our soldiers, but practising battle with their pipes and spears. The officers were Africk and Caribe indifferently; and they seemed to have devised a military language of grunts and yells comprehensible to all: and not so different, perhaps, from the shouts I have heard at home which, while certainly not English, convey a precise meaning to the troops. The women were about their tasks, and it was strange, after slavery, to see them proceeding easily among the men; some of the younger stopped to admire the evolutions of the soldiers, and threw jokes at them or cries of wonder.

'Well,' said Bandele breaking his silence, 'what do you say now?'

'With these, I suppose,' said I in no generous tones, 'you will first capture Lettop, then the islands, and next both the Americas?'

'Bo-bo, your people did, so why not we? And please to remember, for most of us, this is our home.'

'But for all that you need ships, not just frail canoes.'

'N'h – h'n. This is what Daniel would like to see you for.'

The Rebels

DANIEL emerged from a hut and beckoned me. So powerful is our education (if this is the word for the corruption of our minds) in our perpetual superiority, that even now I, a powerless youth, felt his pretensions to glory were absurd. But this sensation did not last me long. For it grew on my reason that his power here was real, and I could also see how, even more than Bandele, he had undergone a profound change not just in posture, but one that was physical. He looked graver, more dangerous and, I thought, tragic.

'And so,' he said, 'now you come back to us. And why then did you run away?'

'Run from where, Daniel?'

'From the Cay, boy. As soon as you see that white sailor on the Cay, you forget us, we who you say your friends, and never harm you.' I said nothing. 'And now you come back,' he said. 'Well, what you hope for now?'

'I come here to take Diana, as you know.'

'Oh! You come to take she! Well: have you arsk her if she want to go? An' you sure is she you come lookin' for, not something else?'

'Why did you steal her?' I asked, speaking as indignantly as I dared.

'And why you steal she from off the Cay? Yeah. Well, I tell you why we take her now. To bring you after us with that ship, an' in a river that is ours and cannot help you.'

'So we have imagined.'

'Oh, you did? Well, you right. But the question is, you see, who goin' to get it: we or Nayle.'

'And when you get the ship, Daniel?'

He looked at me bleakly, as if I were too lost for understanding, too much a prisoner of a life that could never be his, yet was not even my own.

'Then we take an island,' he said quietly.

'An empty one?'

'First. Then one is not empty.'

'You, Daniel? And a few hundred slaves and Indians here?'

'Others will join us.'

'Without guns? In their chains?'

He glared at me a moment, then gave out a little laugh, closing his eyes. 'You know,' he said, 'this slavery and sugar on the islands make you all fat and foolish. Cos when your ancestor first came here, and brought we, they did not ask if it was possible. They did it. But now, what can you do? Only hold on. But a lean man who will take is stronger than a fat man who try hold.'

'But you are becoming a fat man too.'

'Oh. You say I fat?'

'You have the treasure.'

He laughed. 'That's what you tink,' he said. 'That's what Nayle tink, and why he come after we.'

'But you have it.'

'No.'

It was my turn to smile now. 'When you escaped from the Cay, I suppose you threw it in the sea.'

'That's jus' what we do.'

'Did you! And why?'

'Oh! You want to know? Well, boy, suppose I tell you. Bandele find it, and we dig it up. So then a canoe come, with Caribes. So what do we do? Put ourselves in the canoe, or put the gold?'

'Put both.'

'If the weight not too much.'

'Well, you could have come back for the gold.'

'Yeah? An' find Nayle man swarmin' on the Cay, chasin' us to kill?'

'You could have hid it somewhere else on the Cay, and come back later.'

He stared at me. 'I know that what you do, boy,' he said. 'But we, we decide to give it back to the secret where it come from.'

Disbelieving him, I turned ironickal. 'But if you are going to conquer the Caribbean, Daniel, it would have helped you.'

'Oh yes – you sure? All you white come here for is gold, and what it do to you? It ruin an' corrupt you. My gold is different – it out there.'

He pointed at his ragamuffin army. And though at this moment, sucking on his great faith, I half believed that this bandit tribe could conquer the might of five European nations, I must try to dash his hopes: kindly because I feared for him, cruelly because I feared him. 'You cannot do it, Daniel,' I said. 'Never.'

'"Never" a big word. If I not do it, another will. Somebody got to make a start at it.'

There was a shout from the soldiers, who clustered round my three companions from the boat who were brought into the clearing, Charles bound, the two others walking free – their allegiance, it seemed, transferr'd now to the rebel band.

I waited for the murder, as I was waiting for my own. Daniel, seeing my face, said, 'Now, do not you go worry, boy, we not goin' to kill you yet.'

I have read how men, faced with death or even danger, say brave and memorable words. But, 'Well, I hope not,' was all I found to say.

Daniel laughed. 'Not yet, no,' he said. 'We want a heap of informations from you about that ship: how many crew, who they, what weapon, what anchorage she have, what watch is kept. Then you can help us capture it.'

I saw the prisoners being fed, and said in a petulance, 'Well, look – I hunger now.'

'Poor boy! You not a want to see Diana?'

'She is here?'

He pointed to his hut. 'In there. I expeck she like a little chat, and ting, with you as well.'

'So you have ravish'd her!'

Daniel let out a guffaw. 'Boy, you not *know* that woman! Was she ravish me, I tell you!'

'You are bound to say that.'

'Oh, I am? Look around and tell me! Those pretty girls here, Africk and Caribe. You tink I need that dry pale piece?'

'All blacks lust after whites.'

'Yeah, is what you say. But you not ask we our opinion.'

I heard in myself the voice of Mr Newbury. 'You deny there have been black rapes?'

'Not a bit, and I not blame them! But that not desire, man, is revenge!' Here he smiled pleasantly. 'And what do you mean to do with her?' I asked.

'She? Seem like she want to stay with us – you ask her.'

'She cannot love you!'

'Boy, I said "stay", not "love" . . . Nor me love her neither. Slaves do not love, you know. They have century to forget how to . . . But what we do with she, is same what we do with you, boy, and that sailor there.'

I did not like his look, nor want to hear him say more. I turned away, and went inside the hut.

I had expected to find in Diana one of two conditions, considering her fate. The first was (and I confess I hoped for this) a wild indignation and a ravag'd pride, a revolt and determination for revenge. Or the other (which I was prepared to believe possible), a kind of horrid glorifying in her subservience to the slaves: like that of some white Pokohontas, a princess conquering, by her flesh and will, the sullen stupidity of the invaders. But I found neither: for when I saw her, sitting calmly and drinking at some brew they made here, she reminded me instantly of the lesser harlots I had seen in St Laughter, and in the brothel-house of France. She looked coarse, slattern and annoyed; and her face seemed to have lost all the radiance and resolve that made beautiful a nature which was in all else so worthless. But I felt no joy at her diminution, only pangs that what I had loved, had gone; and yet I still felt as much for her, so greatly is any being our idea of them, rather than what they are.

'Oh!' she said, opening an attack before I could my mouth. 'So I suppose you have come gallantly to rescue me!'

'There is but faint hope of that,' said I.

'Aye, faint hope of anything from the faint-hearted. For let me tell you this! Were it not for me, you would have been slain instantly when they took you!'

'How so?'

'How so, fool? Because of the dominion I have over them.'

'You are not now in Meadowsweet, Diana.'

'Oh, Meadowsweet! Who do you think ruled *that* – my father, or was it I?'

'And you rule here too?'

At this, for the first time, she looked abashed. 'I rule that slave and murderer,' she said, 'because I must.' She got up, or rather stagger'd up, and walked about imperially a while in this ramshackle palace. Then she glanced at me and, peering first through the opening, came close and said, 'But now, boy, we must try to deceive them and make off.'

I laughed at this. 'Diana,' I said, 'you have played this trick before. And I believe you think that you will always rule me too.'

She smiled, not to me, but to herself. 'I do not doubt it,' she replied.

'Well, I must admire your conceit, if not your blindness.'

'Blindness! So, boy, are you telling me that *you* have succeeded so brilliantly in your adventures? What have you got that you intended to? All you have won since you sailed here is slavery and a slut's child!' I did not reply and, her breast heaving with rage, she turned her fury from me to others who had offended her immense self-pride. 'Oh, they disgust me!' she cried in a kind of frenzy, that seemed to me to have more of passion than of loathing. 'I cannot wait until I make them suffer for their indignities!'

'You tried to escape these?' She glared at me trembling. 'Did you not go freely from the ship when Mrs Obidiah told you they would be sending for you secretly?'

At this she flung into a fine fury, and crying, 'That you could believe this!' she slapped at me, but I dodged her blow.

'It will not help you,' I said, 'to make an enemy of me now.

She burst into tears that seemed to me not of grief, but at her mortification. And I found her weeping did not touch me, but only caused me to despise her. So I left her then and did not see her much again.

The plans for the attack down to the estuary were perfected by a practice in canoes along the river below the village. In the stream, there was a small island, and this was supposed to be the *Scorpion*, and they manoeuvred round it by day and night; planting 'guards' upon it to detect them, who acted as Nayle's vigilant defenders. Daniel, whom I have called 'the general' in mockery, now proved himself to be one; and I was not amazed at this, because all I learned in the Highlands had persuaded me that the military art, in any man of will and courage, is more one of imagination and good sense, than of a special science; and most of all, in the commander's skill at winning the men's faith and confidence. Charles was kept bound, though I was allowed to visit him to tell what was afoot, and he was not harmed. Nor was I myself hindered, except that I was not allowed outside the village; and if I strayed too far, brought swiftly back by darts from blow-pipes whizzing past my ears. Evidently Daniel thought that I could do them all no harm; and because I had revealed to him all the secrets of the *Scorpion*, he believed me subservient by cowardice, if not by any loyalty. What was his high strategy, I did not know: but there was something impressive in the alliance of these tatter'd warriors of three peoples, in their desperate assurance, and even in their innocence of the might arrayed against them.

At length we set off, like an armada; and parties were sent ahead on foot by either bank, to join with us at the gulf. These landsmen carried tree trunks, and I wondered at this, until I divined that down at the mouth of Wilhelmina, where there was no foliage, they had a plan to construct some kind of a prohibiting boom. It was clear that they depended on surprise, for we moved only at night; though when I saw that Diana and Charles and I were put into the front canoes, I had an uneasy premonition that Daniel might think to use us as hostages to frighten Nayle into surrender: which I well knew would have no effect on him at all.

As we sailed downstream silently, I wondered what counter-plots the admiral (that is, Nayle) was preparing against our general and his troops. I now believed what Daniel said about the treasure, and thought whether Nayle, if he knew of this, would have abandoned his part of the enterprise. But I guessed that he would not; for Nayle was a kind of patriot, and I believe that Daniel had come to mean to him not just the robber of his gold, but a rebellious devil. As for me, I had but one determination: which was to remain neutral in this battle if I could, and flee from both armies.

I had half thought that *Scorpion* might have vanish'd, so much had all my existence become a kind of dream. And here I must mention what may make this feeling of mine more credible, since it might be supposed I could be nothing else than anxious and alert. The Caribes chew at a root which, like opium, renders the senses fickle. For those accustomed to it, it can induce energy and valour, so European soldiers say who have fought with the Caribes. But to a novice, to eat it encourages a kind of misty lassitude and pleasure. I had taken this root at the Caribe village, at first not knowing what it was; but discovering this, to still my alarm I became a lover of it, and, indeed, carried a chunk of it now against my breast.

Rounding the estuary, we saw *Scorpion*, and a sigh rose from the canoes like a soft wind. We beached to make contact with the land parties, a mile or so away from the precious ship. The attack was decided on for dawn.

I was eager to see Daniel's strategy, but dismayed by part of what this was to be. Caribes on the banks, and circling in canoes (armed with their blow-pipes), any captain could have imagined. But what I had not foreseen was that the Caribes, marvellous swimmers, can advance long distances under water, trailing spears, and with knives between their teeth. But my alarm came when I discovered that I was to be the attackers' chief decoy: for I was to sail down openly, in a canoe, upon the side furthest from the land, calling out to the ship, and demanding to speak with Nayle, so that all their attention would be momentarily riveted on me. And Daniel told me, with a chuckle, that he had no fear of my treachery. For the Caribes with their pipes would be observing me from the darkness; and lest that avail insufficiently, he himself would be lying hid in the canoe, with a knife pois'd at my belly. Bandele, meanwhile, would lead the attack out from the shore.

And so we rowed off, I now paddling, and all creeping nearer to the ship: which, until quite close, seemed lonely and deserted, like a hulk; but as we drew up, and the dawn breaking, I could sense men watching, and saw one in the first light: which was Nayle, alert beside the helm, and waiting. The knife prodded me, and knowing not which words to use, I called out, 'Captain! Captain Nayle! There is no more treasure!'

'How say you? Shout up, lad! No what?'

'The treasure, Captain! It is all thrown in the sea!'

A laugh came across the water. 'In the sea, is it? Then we shall fetch it out, for all my treasures have come from out the sea!'

Then I heard another cry, which was, 'Oh, Captain, save me from the slaves!' and this was Diana.

Daniel plunged his knife, but I was ready for this and twisted, catching the wound on my hip. He leapt over, and swam towards the ship: where there fired out a crackling of bursts and flares, and from round about, yells and whistling darts. I turned the canoe towards the sound of Diana's, and ramm'd into it suddenly, upsetting the Caribes who were standing up with both hands on their pipes. I seized a knife from one of them, and chopp'd Charles free; then turned back to *Scorpion*, hoping he could protect her.

Now it was beautiful: yes, far more than fearful, for the battle was so joined, with men clambering, firing, falling, all quite obsess'd. He who has not struggled to death and with it, may wonder at the rapture which overtakes men at arms, and think only of the horror. Yet what man, of all those struggling to take *Scorpion* or save it, would have left the murderous clamour of his own free will?

And it seemed to me also like a kind of fable. Here was the ship, the pride of Europe and its skills; defended by an Englishman whose will and power ruled a motley crew of every race that he had brought here. And swarming about it, hating it yet envious, were the furious dispossessed, fighting to regain their birthright by possession of the white man's floating citadel.

I came alongside and, bleeding, struggled up. In such a confusion of sudden killing, one can move by chance with a strange ease, for all are so intent upon a particular slaughter.

Nayle had gone from the stern, and I thought to spy him up at the prow, beside his great cannon which was roaring, deflected, into the glistening sea. I think he saw me, for a flare lit his face in a grimace. Then, glaring around, he seized upon the cannon, and spun it to fire into his ship. He held up the flare, when from the press a man, I believe Daniel, stabbed at him in the neck, thrusting again fast. But Nayle jabbed his torch into the powder, and the ball tore into the crew, the attackers and the deck, *Scorpion* was ablaze, all were running, and those who could leaping off.

In the sea, half burn'd, I swam and clutch'd on a canoe, and was hauled up by Charles who paddled on. The Caribes were racing, terrified by the exploding boat which glowed like a red skeleton, reflected shuddering in the water. Diana screamed, trying to leap out, but Charles dealt her a blow in the face that robbed her of her senses. I took up another paddle, half sick with loss of blood.

Looking back, I saw more smoke now than fire in a lazy spiral, rising against the mountains. Heads bobbed in the water, and empty crash'd canoes, but others hurrying away. What became of Nayle, or Daniel, I know not; but I expect that Bandele lived, being on land . . .

I owe my life, and so did Diana (for what little worth it is) to the fortitude of the sailor Charles. For she was useless to him, and I half so, but he got us out into the ocean, and pushed our boat on eastward, in shallows beside the coast. I had fainted away when we were picked up and brought in to Lettop . . .

The Prison

ALEXANDER NAIRN was hanged, in the nineteenth year of his life, here in St Laughter, at which place I am Minister of the Presbyterian Church. The account he has left was written, in part of my own urging, at the prison of Joie, our chief town in the island; for there he was awaiting confirmation of the sentence passed on him by Magistrates come out to judge his case from Resurrection. How true his story is, I know not; but he seemed calm enough while he wrote it and, if I questioned him on any particular (such as those that seemed incredible, or evil beyond truth), he assured me it was so, and I thought him well grounded in his facts; though of his opinions I say nothing, preferring that his dead voice should speak of itself. I will add that I have made no alteration to his narration, save in some small points of grammar; and that if I reveal it now (for he confided the papers to me), it is because ten years have passed since his death, and I think few can be harmed by its perusal.

The charges brought against my namesake were threefold: of escaping from slavery, of piracy, and of rebellion. If Alexander's account be credited, he was guilty only of the first; and not even, I would say, guilty of that in the eyes of the Almighty (if one may guess at all They see), since he was enslaved by fraud. As to the piracy, it is true that he sailed with Nayle, though I believe reluctantly; but since Nayle perished (or so we must suppose), we can never be certain on this particular; which, had Nayle been caught, interrogation might have wrung from him. The charge of rebellion I must say I believe absurd; and many others of substance in St Laughter, not otherwise sympathetic to young Nairn, laughed at it too, saying the 'rebel' Daniel, the 'scaped slave, led no revolt that came to anything or, if he did so, was traitor to the Dutch, not us, for his exploits were on their territory. But of this we shall not be certain either; for though ships from our navy, in the course of the recent war with France, have visited the Wilhelmina, and discovered the wreck of *Scorpion*, none knows what befell the upstart Daniel: or, if they do, keep silence.

I think Alexander might have escaped hanging, and been but lashed or made slave again, had any been there to speak for him. True, the seaman Charles did, but as he was a pirate too, and hanged for it, this availed Alexander little. Worse, while none spoke in his favour, one voice that all listened to was raised painfully against him: that of Mrs Wilson, or Diana Newbury as she was then. Her witness was the more deadly not only by what she related, which was horrible enough, but because of the extreme sympathy for the abominations that she suffered, in the minds of the Planters here. She soon left the island, bowed down by further griefs; for her father, Mr Newbury of Meadowsweet, had died during her ravishment by the pirates and then the slaves; and her mother, who was in Europe, succumbed soon after Miss Newbury's arrival there. She then married old Mr Wilson, father to her former lover Horatio, that had been murdered by the slaves, and has become heiress both to Valentine and Meadowsweet. Yet I doubt if she will return here, for both plantations now have Overseers to manage them.

It was because such a length of time elapsed between his sentence and its final confirmation, that Alexander was able to set down his story. On charges so grave (to which there was later added that of murder), there had to be further judgement by the Governor in Resurrection; and His Excellency, perhaps out of some pity (or that love of officials for delay), referred the whole case to London for a final decision. Enquiries had also to be made about the boy's tale that he had respectable relatives in Ayrshire; and in this I tried to assist him too, even writing to the Moderator in Edinburgh. But no ease came to him from thence; and when more than a year had passed, we learned in St Laughter that the sentence must be fulfilled.

In prison, besides writing, the boy read diligently from books that I provided, seeming to prefer the historical to the religious; though I pressed these divine works on him, thinking he might have greater need of Heavenly wisdom, than in that of Earth. He also questioned me closely about the Caribbean, and of how things had come to pass here as they had; in which I assisted him as honestly as I was able.

Besides the writing of his tale, which he did not live to complete (for he was stopp'd short of the trial), Alexander had but one other preoccupation. He revealed to me that he had once lain shamefully with a slave girl, and got her a child; and he beseeched me to try to seek her out, and assist his boy if I was able. But this, in conscience, I was obliged to refuse him. For there was not only the double sin (I mean of fornication, and lying with a slave), but experience has taught us here that it is best a slave child, if gotten by a European, should know nothing of its ancestry. He was cast down when I told him that, before God, this was my opinion; and would not speak with me for several weeks. But then he soften'd, and said to me with a sort of sigh (which I confess touch'd me), 'Well, I shall leave a descendant in St Laughter, and if they do not find him, they cannot harm him further.'

There remains one particular concerning which, to round out my account truthfully, I should say something. Supposing Nayle had left a treasure on the Cay; supposing the escaped slaves had found it and, instead of casting it into the sea as they averred, had hidden it in some other place upon the island, then it must still be there. Curious of this, I went there with some sailors – all honest Presbyterians – after the boy's death; for I had the thought that if anything might be found, I could build the new kirk that we need here so desperately, for all the tithes go to the Anglicans. But though we rummag'd about for several days, we discover'd nothing.

When news of his fate reached him, I enjoined on Alexander to confess all his sins to me, and let me pray with him, so that he might hope to meet fitly with his Redeemer. But he told me his writing was confession enough; and when I rebuked him, said no more, so I desisted. I deem this a failure in my Ministry; but must say I believe it due more to the boy's obstinate spirit than to any lack of zeal on my behalf; for even when he was first brought in shackles in St Laughter, he did not ask for me, and I must seek him out persistently. Nor did he complain, in prison, if I stayed away; though he seemed to welcome me if I came, and was ever eager for the books.

I had long nourished a suspicion which, in his last days, I felt I must reveal to him: which was that, since he said his father was a Highlander, and a Papist, he might have some hankerings there; in which case, said I, against all my best principle, and even imperilling my own salvation, I was prepared to send secretly to the island France, and fetch over a priest. But he said no; and when I asked if there was, then, no final comfort that he hoped for, he smiled a little (to my surprise, and grief I must confess), and asked could I bring to him from Resurrection a black female called Mrs Obidiah: who he said was a notorious witch that should be burned. At this impiety, I left him in a rage: may I be forgiven.

He met death bravely, being hanged in the square at Joie, and before a scant multitude, for it was early morning.

Alexander Yule, D D
Joie, St Laughter
1762